WHALEFALL

WHALEFALL

A NOVEL

DANIEL KRAUS

Entertainment
BOOKS

NEW YORK LONDON TORONTO SYDNEY NEW DELHI

An Imprint of Simon & Schuster, Inc.
1230 Avenue of the Americas
New York, NY 10020

First MTV Books/Atria Books hardcover edition August 2023

ATRIA BOOKS and colophon are registered trademarks of Simon & Schuster, Inc.

For information about special discounts for bulk purchases, please contact Simon & Schuster Special Sales at 1-866-506-1949 or business@simonandschuster.com.

The Simon & Schuster Speakers Bureau can bring authors to your live event. For more information or to book an event, contact the Simon & Schuster Speakers Bureau at 1-866-248-3049 or visit our website at www.simonspeakers.com.

Interior design by Jill Putorti

Jacket art by Will Staehle

Manufactured in the United States of America

1 3 5 7 9 10 8 6 4 2

Library of Congress Cataloging-in-Publication Data
Names: Kraus, Daniel, 1975–author.
Title: Whalefall : a novel / Daniel Kraus.
Description: First MTV Books/Atria Books hardcover edition. |
New York : MTV Entertainment Books, 2023.
Identifiers: LCCN 2022059573 (print) | LCCN 2022059574 (ebook) |
ISBN 9781665918169 (hardcover) | ISBN 9781665918176 (paperback) |
ISBN 9781665918183 (ebook)
Subjects: LCGFT: Thrillers (Fiction) | Novels.
Classification: LCC PS3611.R3757 W53 2023 (print) | LCC PS3611.R3757 (ebook) |
DDC 813.6–dc23/eng/20221213
LC record available at https://lccn.loc.gov/2022059573
LC ebook record available at https://lccn.loc.gov/2022059574

ISBN 978-1-6659-1816-9
ISBN 978-1-6659-1818-3 (ebook)

To ten writers who changed how I write:

Megan Abbott

Richard Adams

P. Djèlí Clark

Carol J. Clover

Joseph P. DeSario

Ralph Ellison

Junji Ito

Kathe Koja

Grace Metalious

Herman Wouk

If this whale be a king, he is a very sulky looking fellow.

—HERMAN MELVILLE, *MOBY-DICK*

TRUTH

3000 PSI

Highway 1 drones. Cypress trees roar. Gulls shriek in squadrons. Yet all Jay Gardiner hears is his father awakening the family at six a.m. Weekdays, weekends, holidays, the man's blood so attuned to tidal patterns that he gets up without an alarm to begin the bedroom invasions, cowbelling his coffee cup.

Sleepers, arise!

Mitt Gardiner's been dead a year now, but his foghorn will be startling Jay from sleep for the rest of his life, he's sure of it.

Jay loves his mom, though, and his sisters, they're okay. So there's guilt. For refusing their reasonable requests throughout the whole ugly saga. Mom, Nan, and Eva have therapists now and talk about "closure." Jay's not sure he believes in therapy. He definitely doesn't believe in closure. People aren't doors. They're whole floor plans, entire labyrinths, and the harder you try to escape, the more lost inside them you become.

Jay's seventeen years deep into the maze, too late to backtrack.

His car sheds rust scabs as he grovels it along the cinnamon shoulder of Highway 1. A white cloud parachutes over the road, mist from ocean waves he hears but can't see. No open parking spots. Weird. This isn't Huntington Beach. There are no fudge shops, no bikini boutiques, only the Santa Lucia Mountains. Early August, quarter to eight in the morning, Monastery Beach should be a ghost town, aside from Catholic cars tootling up the hill for mass at the Carmelite Monastery.

Jay uses the first four swear words he thinks of. He should go home, pick a different day. Crows puff and flap inside his rib cage in stern disapproval. This sets his heart lobbing, his scalp sweating. He's psyched himself up so hard for this, doom metal tunes and coffee, that the idea of quitting nauseates him. If he leaves now, that's it, he'll never come back. To people who know him, he'll forever be the shit scraped off Mitt Gardiner's shoe.

Over the berm are the waters where Mitt died.

Closure, no. But signposts through the labyrinth? Maybe.

"You're doing the dive, Jay," he says.

Moving forward is the only way out. He's ashamed how badly his mother misses him. His sisters are furious with him. Seems like no one in Monterey thinks he even deserves the name *Gardiner* after how he allowed his father to suffer without him.

This dive could change all of it.

Unclenched, his jaw lets in the familiar tastes of salt, sand, and fear.

He knows another place to park, a side route to the beach.

U-turn. A great blue heron objects with a swoop as dawn light blinds. Different from dusk light, though both feel like kinds of snares. Mitt disagreed. Jay thinks back on it. He's thought of nothing but his father all morning.

2015

"Steinbeck called this 'the hour of the pearl.'"

It's dusk, the dusk of dusk, an unblurred luster. Dad's talking about John Steinbeck's *Cannery Row*. You can't go two feet in downtown Monterey without the book being bragged about on street signs and from shopwindows. Like the sardine factory ruins on the Row itself, Steinbeck's novel evokes a simpler, pitiless time. Qualities Mitt Gardiner values. To him, modern Monterey is a boil seeping tourist pus over a coastline that should have been left to the fish-stinking folk who worked it.

Jay, age ten, disagrees. The Row is electrifying. Music pumped from crunchy restaurant speakers. Fried food in the wind, outdoor magicians. Ice cream splats on the sidewalk that Dad says look like blood but make Jay hungry.

"'When time stops and examines itself,' he wrote."

They are waiting in a hotel parking lot. Dad's current gig is scraping scum off the hotel's pier. In five minutes his boss will show up and fire him. It's Dad's attitude. You can't chew out guests, Mitt, even when they toss a plastic cup into the bay. Dad's twisting *Cannery Row* inside huge hands. Dad's no reader. This book's the sole exception, his source of workaday psalms.

He hands the book to Jay like it's religion. Jay doesn't hate *Cannery Row* yet, but after teachers force him to read it in sixth, eighth, and tenth grades, he will. A chunk of pages falls out and is stolen by the wind, yellow swallows to join the black cormorants lording over the cannery ruins. Dad watches them soar.

"That's all right. Every hour of the pearl, you realize you've lost pages too. More and more pages until"—he whistles—"you're all gone."

Dad plucks another page free with his right hand, the one missing half the ring finger. Lets the page fly away, gone like his job. He taps the book, fat from water damage.

"What happens when you die in the ocean: bloat."

3000 PSI

Five hundred feet north is the Bay School Parent Co-Op Preschool, a low magenta building notched into tall green trees. It's closed, red playground plastic faded a cataract pink, no scrambling rugrats. Jay's glad. Doesn't have time for jealousy. His only childhood playgrounds were kelpy piers, moss-velveted docks, boats that stank of sulfur.

He steers off Highway 1 into the school lot, tires munching fallen leaves. The hell? Cars here too. Only four, but that's four more than expected. Jay parks, glad for the mask of shade. The pickup truck to his right sports two blue logos, NOAA and NMFS—National Oceanic and Atmospheric Administration and National Marine Fisheries Service.

"You gotta be shitting me."

Jay strikes the steering wheel with open palms. Just his luck. Ninety-nine days out of a hundred, a diver could drop off Monastery Beach without a single witness. Today there's some kind of, what? Environmental disaster? He looks left and his skin bakes hotter: an orange-striped SUV with the words UNITED STATES COAST GUARD.

"The *fuck*."

Mitt Gardiner hated a lot of things, people, ideas, and philosophies, but nothing needled him more than what he called the Dirty CGs. Jay hates agreeing with his father on anything; each time is an infection. But discharging his passed-down distrust of the coast guard would be like extracting his own spleen.

Jay doesn't need a therapist to tell him he's being stupid. Someone might have drowned on Monastery last night and the coast guard is picking up the pieces. Jay's misgivings come from how reliably the Dirty CGs upset his father, how often he bore witness to Mitt's fury. He recalls sniffling tears while Mitt harassed a Dirty CG for ticketing some petty violation.

You're going to tell me what's right for the ocean, you pencil pusher? I was born on the water! (Not even true, according to Granny Gardiner. She went into labor on a boat, but Mitt was delivered at a hospital like an ordinary human—how humiliating.)

Anytime Mitt went off, Jay alone was there to absorb it, to tremble and cry, then suffer Mitt's disgust for Jay's infant reactions. No, not alone. Not quite. Gulls, otters, sea lions, sharks, even the occasional whale filled out the audience.

Those beasts never flinched from Mitt's tirades.

Jay won't either. Not anymore.

If the NOAA and CG are here, they may try to stop him from diving.

But if a diver is crafty, he might not be spotted in the first place.

3000 PSI

Jay drove with his wetsuit half-on. He hasn't missed the rubbery grip of the neoprene on his legs and crotch. The top half of the ebony suit pools at his waist like peeled skin. The suit is a Henderson, sun-faded, coral-scraped, that tricky zipper. Crap condition, but that's the case with all his gear. He had to dig it out of the bins he's been hauling around for two years. It feels flimsier than he remembered, scuba toys, not the real deal.

Jay gets out of the car. First thing, his hood. He pulls it on, ears gluing flat to his skull, the neoprene bib overlaying his scrawny sternum. He fishes his hands into the wetsuit arms. It tugs his arm hair. He forgot how it stings. Once on, the Henderson's heavy as clay, seven millimeters thick for cold Monterey Bay waters. If the water temp hits fifty-eight this time of year, that's lucky. Jay reaches over his back, feels for the two-foot zipper tether, and takes it with both hands. Jay doesn't believe in God but prays like he does.

Three years back, he cracked the zipper head on a boat rail while making a January drop at East Pescadero Pinnacle. He hand-signaled his father to surface and in open air removed his regulator to report that his back was exposed. Mitt's stare was blank as the side of a machete. A busted zipper is your own fault. Mitt dropped, Jay followed. It was the coldest dive of his life, the rigid sea rawing his body, his teeth chattering off his mouthpiece plastic, amplified through the plates of his frozen skull.

The zipper is the only piece of equipment Jay repaired for today. He didn't fix it yesterday at the dive shop when he got his tank re-filled. He spent as little time there as possible. Everyone at area shops revered Mitt Gardiner, local legend, walking tome of maritime lore. Their eyes forever bright for the old diver's approval while Jay, use-less infant, withered. Dive bros knew Mitt drank—hell, it was how you pumped the best stories from the guy's gut—but they didn't know he was a *drunk*, a periodic jailbird, a malcontent who couldn't hold a job more than a couple years and acted like it was a testament to his principles.

Principles: a nifty excuse for being an asshole.

Jay isn't ignored by dive bros anymore. Now he's despised. Some-how the story got out: Mitt's long illness, the son's selfish refusal to ease his pain. They don't know what the real Mitt was like. They don't have any idea.

So Jay took his wetsuit to Mel's Shoes in Del Rey Oaks and dealt with Mel, a thousand-year-old dude who didn't know a dive skin from a farmer john but ran his wrinkled fingertips over the wetsuit zip-per like a tongue over teeth. Now Jay yanks the tether and the zip-per roller-coasters the curve of his spine, sealing him off inside. He exhales.

"If there's a God, Mel, God bless you."

2017

"You get in a jam, shoe repairmen are your best friends. Get to know your local cobbler, Jay. Those old coots have skills like no one else alive."

Dad says this while stepping into the bright red vulcanized rubber of a full-body drysuit with PVC face shield. Looks cool, like's he's off to battle aliens. He's not. They're at Pepper Hills Golf Links, a twenty-minute drive from home that feels like twenty million. Unbroken seas of trimmed grass. Clubhouse of dove-colored wood. Dad's current job? Part of a three-person crew diving for golf balls at the bottom of Pepper Hills ponds. *White gold*, Dad says. At twenty-five cents a ball? Jay's skeptical, but Dad says it adds up.

The other two divers suiting up are eighteen. Too close to Jay's twelve for him not to blush.

Dad never shuts up about the great jobs he's held. Abalone collecting, oil-rig work, diving for herring roe in Alaska; he's got a topographic tattoo of the forty-ninth state on his thigh. Nan and Eva always roll their eyes at these stories, while Mom places food on the table, super quiet. Jay thinks it's because these stories are pre-Mom, back when Dad roamed and dived wherever he pleased, back when he was—there's no other way to put it—happy.

It makes Jay feel deranged. Dad's got everything a man could want. A wife who dotes on him despite his defects. Two daughters to trade playful insults with. A son to torture.

Apparently it's not enough.

Since Jay started having memories to call his own, Dad's jobs haven't squared with the reverence he gets from local divers. Sewage outfall inspection: checking where shit feeds from pipes into the ocean. Refurbishing pier pilings in plastic or cement. Scrubbing barnacles, moss, and Bryozoa off boat hulls for local yachties, a buck a foot, then barfing in the ditch from the copper and cyanide in the paint.

Dad's fifty-two years old. Pepper Hills is his lowliest job yet.

3000 PSI

Jay pops the trunk. His BCD, buoyancy compensating device, has seen better days, but only scarcely: Mitt Gardiner had superstitions about new gear. His came secondhand, and Jay's third. This one's an old Oceanic, a thick black vest using a puzzlement of clips and pockets to corral a tentacular drape of hoses.

He buckled the air tank into the BCD before he left but gives it a double check. It's only his life, right? Two black straps tightened around the cylinder with cams. A safety strap looped to the tank's K valve. It's the only air source Jay's got, a banged-up 120-cubic-foot cylinder, steel instead of aluminum. The thicker wetsuits required for Monterey Bay's cold make a diver so buoyant it helps to have steel's extra density.

Another fifteen pounds stowed in the BCD pockets would be ideal. But Jay's storage bins yielded only a couple of five-pound dive weights. The last thing he did before departing was to raid the Tarshish house for that final five pounds. In the kitchen drawer, he found a motherlode of Duracell batteries. Quick google search. One D battery equals 180 grams; 403 grams equals one pound.

He busted free twelve D batteries and, to make up the change, a handful of loose AAs and a single 9-volt. Now his BCD pockets are chipmunk-cheeked. Feels weird. Jay hopes they hold.

Sixty degrees tops but, man, he's sweating, skin greasy inside the wetsuit. Jay hoists the octopus retainer from the trunk and screws it

to the tank valve. Four hoses droop. He connects the inflater to the
BCD and sweeps the other danglers to the side. He slides the whole
thing to the edge of the trunk. Time to strap on. Once he's wearing
seventy pounds of this stuff, it'll be too much trouble to turn back.
Right?

Seventy. Even now, the sheer weight of it shames him.

2017

"We didn't have big, heavy stab jackets when I started. We had heavy-ass tanks that sunk your ass fast. No wetsuits either. We had long-sleeved shirts and coveralls. We never logged dives. We dove for now. What's your certification?"

Jay, twelve, on a pier, salami sandwiches in wax paper. Hewey's there, too, paying a kid to gas up the boat engine. Hewey is Dad's best friend. Maybe his only friend. A former dentist, he now spends all waking hours boating and fishing, chubby with life vests. Hewey can't swim. It's bonkers. The guy's, what? Sixty? Seventy? Jay's never been able to pin it. Could be a hundred. He loves the old man. Why Hewey puts up with Mitt, he'll never know.

"Open Water I," Jay replies.

Mitt laughs, a rare thing. Oddly enough, his big square head is carved by laugh lines, the right parenthesis hatched by an old spearfishing scar. There must have been a time when Mitt Gardiner's world was rife with things to laugh about. He's over six feet tall, hands the size of tennis racquets, body etched in nautical tattoos, no fat, though signs of aging have emerged. A curve to the shoulders, slackening chest muscles, fingers kind of shaky. Still bigger and stronger than Jay will ever be.

"Boat's gassed." Hewey's shadow is deep and cool. "Don't be mean, Mitt."

Mitt ignores him. "Open Water I. Open Water II. Deep Diving.

Night Diving. Wreck Diving. Cave Diving. You know what kind of classes we had? We had a drill sergeant who gave us goggles painted over with black paint and made us do laps till we got so tired he had to fish us out with a net. You swam long enough? Boom. Congratulations. You're a diver."

3000 PSI

Jay sits on the bumper. Left arm laced through the BCD vest, right arm. Motion is instantly limited, that straitjacket pinch. Waist strap, thick velcro. Cummerbund and chest strap, two dog-collar snaps. All right, here we go, time to stand. Jay wonders if two years away from diving has whittled his spine to a twig.

He leans forward, shifting the weight from the car trunk. Feels like a Toyota Corolla on his back. He pictures himself face-planting into the dirt, pinned by his own gear until a Dirty CG found him. Clench the thighs, now, piston the legs—and Jay's up, only a second unsteady before he remembers how to be a mule. It's not the fifty-pound tank he carries, not the fifteen pounds of weights and batteries. It's seventeen years of being Mitt Gardiner's son, the expectations and disappointments, all of it on his back one more time.

Muscle memory: his sweaty hands redo the straps for an upright posture. His knees judder, and it's got nothing to do with the weight. *This is called trauma*, he thinks. Maybe he ought to give in to Mom, Nan, and Eva and reconsider that therapist.

Move, move. Jay bends a knee to swipe his diving mask from the trunk. There's a vial of baby shampoo cradled in it, and he smears the pink goo on the inside of the faceplate. Mask defogging agents are cheap, but Mitt never met an official product he didn't feel he could best with a homemade solution. More than the gear, the shampoo's jasmine scent takes him back.

2016

He's eleven, in Dad's thirteen-foot, Big Bird–yellow Malibu kayak, rubbing shampoo into his little mask's silicone, and he asks Dad if this is the same shampoo Mom washed his hair with when he was a baby. It's the last time he'll ask a question so guaranteed to infuriate. Dad looks appalled, like Jay asked which My Little Pony he liked best.

"If your mother listened to me, you would have stung your eyes with the regular stuff and got all your crying out back then."

It rips the smile off Jay's face. He cries too much, and he knows it. Seems like once a day he suffocates inside a cage of hot, hitching tears. He doesn't know why. He only knows Dad grits his teeth through each episode like it's a personal insult. Jay detects no masculinity inside himself. He clings to his mother's apron, literally. He has a blankie. He's too small. *Skinny as a girl*, Mitt likes to accuse over dinner, pushing plates of food across the table until they collide with Jay's.

3000 PSI

Jay hasn't shed tears in six years. Not even at Mitt's funeral.

He takes the final items from the trunk: two fins and a fine-grade mesh bag. He clips the bag to his BCD. Should use a bolt snap hook, but when he dug out all his dive gear, he couldn't find a single one. Instead, he attaches the bag with a boat snap he borrowed from his friend Chloe Tarshish's schoolbag.

Smart divers don't use boat snaps. They call them "suicide clips," in fact, for their lethal tendency to snag onto anything they touch.

Jay slams the trunk. So be it.

A suicide clip for the place Mitt Gardiner died by suicide.

Jay should have seen it coming the day he learned of the illness.

2021

"Jay. Baby. Your dad's got cancer."

The first thing Jay feels is offended by Mom's quavering tone, her obvious expectation that Jay will break down and rush home, everything that happened between him and his dad forgotten. As if contracting cancer is a deed so selfless it erases everything past. The second thing he feels is stupor. Mitt Gardiner, human sequoia, sick?

"What kind?"

"It's mesothelioma. It's in the lining over his lungs. I've been trying to get him to go to the doctor for months. He's been coughing up blood, having trouble breathing. His whole neck and chest's swollen up. Jay, you don't know."

"Isn't metho— Isn't that caused by asbestos?"

"They told me it happens to scuba divers, too. Especially near Monterey. Especially the older ones who used to dive without wetsuits. I guess there's lots of natural asbestos here. Maybe in those old canneries, too."

Mom doesn't throw knives on purpose, but this one slips her hand and strikes Jay in the lungs, a hint of his own mesothelioma fate, maybe. He feels faint. He drops himself to the floor, out of sight of the carefree Tarshishes. He's enough of a hassle staying with his friend's family; they don't need his drama, too.

"What's the— I mean, how long . . ."

Tears break Mom's levies. "Could be a year. Maybe two. Maybe more if we're lucky."

Pause. Expectant. What is Jay supposed to say? He's kept away thoughts of Dad for five months, ever since he left home. Pictures fan through his mind, but they're all from August 1, 2020, the last time Jay saw Mitt, on the deck of *Sleep*. Colliding with the cancer news, the images hurt. Mom sniffles like she feels it, too.

"Jay, come home. We need you to come home."

3000 PSI

Home? No. Jay's headed the other direction.

At the top of the parking lot is the Carmel Meadows Trailhead. Warning signs all over. No campfires. No leashless dogs. No fishing. All wildlife and plants protected. The largest sign shouts *DANGER— INTERMITTENT WAVES OF UNUSUAL SIZE AND FORCE— WADING AND SWIMMING UNSAFE.*

Jay is past being warned. He tromps through the gate, top-heavy, anvil-footed, eyes to the terrain so he doesn't go boom. If Highway 1 hadn't been a car lot, he would have taken the short route up the beach's berm. The signage there is even shoutier. *DON'T BE THE NEXT VIC-TIM! DO NOT ATTEMPT RESCUE! AT LEAST 30 PEOPLE HAVE DIED AT THIS BEACH!* One fool per year, Mitt used to say. He loved to proclaim Monastery as America's most dangerous beach.

When it came to offing himself, what other choice was there?

Dirt snickers under each step of Jay's bare feet. To his left, a rental property peeking from the oak grove. To his right, low ochre hills of golden grass dotted with tufted weeds and stiff shrubs. Nothing between but open air. Five minutes up the trail is a bracelet of fancy Carmel Meadows homes. A rich old lady with a dog is going to limp over the hill any second, any second.

Jay tenses but can't feel it over the wetsuit's tenser grip. You can't really hide in diving gear. Might as well be wearing a suit of armor.

Ninety seconds later, his luck's still holding. He thuds across two footbridges, hooks left. A downslope, then he's hidden; release the old ladies with dogs! Protected, Jay transforms. The Henderson relaxes over his elbows and knees. The Oceanic molds to his vertebrae. The octopus hoses pat his shoulders as comfortably as Mom. Soothing whispers from all around—spindrift, wild rye.

This is what diving could have been like. What water could have been like. If he hadn't been bullied into both with the martial fanfare of *Sleepers, arise!*

Five more steps and pennants of mist billow away. There it is, the beach, Mitt's graveyard, its rock jaws wide like it's hungry for the ocean itself.

3000 PSI

Fog blankets the bays in the morning, exhaled from green mountains. Burns off by noon most days, but Jay learned as a kid not to be fooled by a silver sky. It'll roast you. He withstands its glare in a standstill swelter, breath caught like it is anytime he sees the licking gray froth, the buck and boil, the guttural suck and spilling stew of Monastery Beach.

Divers called it "Mortuary Beach" for a reason.

Must have dived these waters a dozen times with Mitt. Never alone. Mitt made him promise to never solo it until he was fully grown.

Is he fully grown now? Few would say so. Mitt's diving acolytes sure wouldn't. Six days ago, walking down Fremont, a dive bro—obvious from his neoprene stink and huge watch—spat on Jay's shoe. *Prick*, the dive bro muttered, thinking he knew everything about Mitt, the great diver, and Jay, the spiteful son.

Maybe the dive bro knew enough. Jay can't go on like this. He's got twelve more months before college, whatever college might look like. Twelve more months to be spat on.

A humble crescent of sand is all Monastery Beach is, stretching between Carmel-by-the-Sea and Point Lobos State Natural Reserve. A twenty-minute stroll for tourists who happen by en route to San Francisco, a percentage of whom will stand with their backs to the water for photos, get swatted by a sleeper wave, and be dragged under by the backwash. It was fit for experienced divers only, and even they had to respect the hidden trough just inside the surf line that, if they didn't choose their entry right, might roll them over and over, a morsel softened for swallowing.

The true wonder, maybe the true horror, comes later, twelve nautical miles into the blue: Monterey Canyon, a ninety-mile-long, mile-deep abyss the size of the Grand Canyon, a frigid black haven for the world's strangest beings. A spindly stem called Carmel Canyon points at Monastery Beach like the Grim Reaper's finger. What is it trying to say?

Jay thinks of AP English, Dante's *Inferno*, the inscription over the gates of hell: *Abandon Hope All Ye Who Enter Here.* Jay's murmur is as soft as surf.

"Oughta just add it to the signs."

3000 PSI

There's a set of wooden stairs, but the ocean air has chewed them up. The steps, about fifteen, are helixed, wrung like a towel. Jay starts down, and the first step punches a bolt of pain from his heel to his pelvis. Under this much gear, an eight-inch drop feels like eight feet.

He tightens his lower back and keeps going. These steps tilt west. Those steps tilt east. The final step is warped at a seesaw angle. Jay slides down it, off the lower edge. His feet plant ankle-deep in the beach's distinctive round granules of sand.

Jay takes five steps, the fifth over a seven-foot carcass of kelp that looks like a decomposing dolphin. Now he can see past the point of the rental property, a macabre fence holding back the exposed roots of a giant tree. Way over on the south end of the beach, a commotion.

Two large banks of lights, a tonnage of chugging generators. A bulldozer crawls over the western berm, shovel-mouthed like some Monterey Canyon monster. Thirty or forty people, too, the drivers of all those cars.

"Shit."

Jay ducks behind the half-uprooted tree. Eyelines blocked. The weight of his tank pitches him at the fence. He barely stays upright. He's panting. The wetsuit's thick, but his heart pounds through it. If the Dirty CGs spot him, they'll prevent him from diving. He can't let that happen. His family, the respect of the community, it all rides on this, showing what he can do—what he can do *without* Mitt Gardiner.

Jay focuses on the tide. It skims into the cove in long, curling cones that atomize under their own weight, strike down, scurry like albino snakes, and gasp in pleasure as they are sucked back into the sea between jagged black rocks.

This rubble is one reason divers never drop from this pocket of Monastery. One bad foothold and you're down. But the boulders only extend some twenty feet. Jay shouts self-help that no one but he can hear through the ocean booms.

"Get through it fast. If you fall, fall forward. Then kick hard. Get through the danger zone before the next set of waves."

The orders sound like Mitt, so Jay does what Mitt never did and adds some optimism.

"You got this, Jay! Sixty seconds and you're through! Like riding a bike!"

He'll be visible for a few seconds before a rocky pile conceals him. He bends his knees. Regrips his fins. Blows five quick exhales to pump himself up. Holds his mask in his left hand. With his right, he tugs a final time on the mesh bag. The suicide clip chimes. No matter how rough this entry, Jay can't lose the bag.

How else is he going to carry his father's remains?

2021

In a way, he's been carrying his whole family's remains for the twelve months he's been living with friends. It's a big ask during a pandemic. The isolation has been rough on all his friends, but Jay suspects it's been roughest on him, without his family there to rely on. He's a professional foster kid, forever trying to fit in with his hosts, to adhere to whatever Covid protocols they follow or disregard. His sinuses ache from all the nasal swabs. It's exhausting, and lonely, and offers too much time to think. Throwing himself into schoolwork is all that has helped.

Outdoors is the only real place he can breathe. It's a Wednesday morning when he steps outside for sun between virtual classes and finds Hewey standing by the Tarshish mailbox, in safari hat and Covid mask, belt too high, hands in pockets. The presence of Hewey's car doesn't make his appearance feel less supernatural.

The second Jay sees him, he knows. The August air goes thick as seaweed. Jay wishes, maybe for the first time ever, he were in the ocean, so he could float over to Hewey, no problem, instead of falling to the lawn on jellyfish legs.

Hewey helps him up. Pulls Jay into his arms. The lax crepe of his hands. The grapey funk of his cologne. The gold chain hard under his half-buttoned shirt. Jay wasn't taught how to hug men, but he's doing it, and it feels like he could give all his weight to Hewey and the old man would hold him up.

"I'm sorry, son."

Jay nods into Hewey's shoulder, afraid to say anything, because what if there's a sob in his throat? What if that sob dislodges more? Hewey's arms feel like the shoulder straps of Jay's BCD.

"It was suicide. I need to tell you that straight up."

Jay nods again. He figured. Last he heard, Dad was out of the hospital, all medical options exhausted.

"We were on my rowboat, son. He threw himself over. I don't know how I feel about that. But that's what happened. I told your mom I wanted to be the one to tell you."

Jay stands straight. Emotion bottled. He's proud of that. Hewey is smiling, but old eyelids, Jay has noticed, can't clamp down on tears. Jay doesn't fault Hewey for the suicide, and he adores Hewey for knowing he wouldn't.

"Dad used you to get out there. He knew you can't swim."

Hewey smiles. Angelic. "Never quit breaking my balls about it."

Jay laughs. What a gift at a moment like this. Hewey takes off his safari hat. Wipes sweat. Jay's heart goes out to him. The old man lost his best friend today off the side of his boat. There must be grief, even guilt. He carries that weight for Jay. Hewey gestures at his car.

"Will you come see your mom?"

Jay nods. Doesn't fetch his wallet, doesn't say a word to Chloe. They get in.

Only after the engine makes a distracting roar does Jay ask.

"Where'd it happen?"

"Monastery."

Hewey's Jewish but has a plastic St. Christopher figure glued to his dash. The patron saint of travel. Jay touches it. There's a flaw in the molding. St. Christopher looks like he's winking.

3000 PSI

You don't spend most your life diving without learning what the ocean does to corpses. Mitt Gardiner would have drawn large scavengers. Probably sharks. Six months from the outset, his corpse would be picked clean, a skeleton. The fact that his bones haven't been spotted by divers suggests they slid between rocks or inside vegetation. Jay hopes to find his dad's skull, but he'll take what he can get. A femur. A few ribs. A handful of finger bones like dice. The proper, legal burial of Mitt's remains, not that sham of a plot in Moss Landing, might provide the mystical "closure" yearned for by his mom and sisters, who then might welcome Jay back into the fold.

For Jay, it'll prove to everyone in the Monterey Bay area that he isn't a worthless son, that he was never needlessly cruel to the great Mitt Gardiner.

What do they know about cruelty?

Last night Jay dreamed of his father's bones, buttery in a nest of purple kelp, bejeweled with red sea slugs like holiday lights. The bones were soft in his hands, a gentle touch he never got from Mitt and therefore never gave back. He slid them against his cheek. He kissed them. He woke up tasting marrow. Funny, it tasted like tears.

3000 PSI

Jay inflates his BCD all the way. He's been worried about the Schrader valve. Delicate thing, subject to sand clogging, salt corrosion. But the vest inflates; good, positive buoyancy. He needs to be able to float if Monastery starts to roll him.

He reaches over his head, cranks the knob of the tank valve. A hissy sigh. That's good; that's air. He checks his scuffed instrument console. The compass does a dizzy spin. The black hand of his depth gauge is at 0, but the red hand holds the max depth of the last dive he made two years ago, 62 feet.

Elkhorn Dive Center in Santa Cruz did him solid. The pressure gauge rests right at 3000 psi. Jay works the regulator under his lips and breathes, and relearns the taste of plastic, the profile of his bite marks. He's breathing too fast and tries to slow it but can't stop his eyes from checking the pressure gauge again. Just like that, down to 2977 psi.

Don't waste air where you don't need it, Mitt used to say.

Even here at the ocean's teeth, Jay can't escape the reprimands.

One way or the other, Mitt Gardiner always swallowed him alive.

2022

How do you escape your father's closing jaws?

You get away. All the way across town, if you can.

Chloe Tarshish lives in Pebble Beach, one of the country's top fifty wealthiest zip codes. Jay's been at the Tarshish place a whole year, the best run he's had. Chloe's parents told him if he cleared out their four-seasons room he could stay there. The room already had a futon, and soon the Tarshishes bought him a yard-sale desk for homework. The Tarshishes are cool. They project foreign films and listen to experimental music. They let their kids watch anything they want and when they caught Chloe looking at porn, everyone just gave her shit.

The Tarshishes are good about Mom, too, chatting her up when she calls to check on Jay, accepting her bank transfers to pay for Jay's needs and never being weird about it, assuring Mom that Jay's fine and agreeing that, no, it's not ideal for a teen boy to live apart from his family, but it's better than having him on the streets, right?

Before the Tarshishes, Jay lived with Tekla Nguyen for five months, Mandy Mapes for three, Evie Nowacek for one, Chet Branch for three really bad days, and Faye Kimmerer for the crucial first fourteen weeks after leaving home. Five of the six are girls. Jay's guy friends can't compute how he didn't get any action from these chicks, but he didn't. He's not getting any from Chloe, either. Jay's not gay, he thinks, at least not mostly, but he prefers the company of women. Always has.

It was one more thing about him to humiliate Dad.

He'd just moved in with the Tarshishes when Dad died. After the cemetery service, Nan and Eva cornered him like two zombies, pleading for him to return home, look at what he was doing to Mom, think how lonely she'll be in that house without Dad. Jay couldn't verbalize that he was too ashamed to cavalierly return the moment his antagonist was gone—it smacked of cowardice. The excuse he gave his sisters was that he was unwilling to upset the winning formula of perfect grades he'd established at the Tarshish home.

He had big plans, he told them. Graduate in the top 5 percent of his class. Get a forestry degree from Berkeley, a job at Yellowstone.

His past is the only undertow. Before going nomad, Jay lived for fifteen years in Seaside, a west Monterey suburb, in a small, one-story, coral-colored house with a red-stone lawn overlooking a trailer park. The house Mom grew up in.

If you mentioned that, though, Dad got mad. Young Jay didn't know why, but his sisters said it was emasculating. What's that mean? It means cutting off Dad's balls. What's *that* mean? It's a metaphor for money. Nan and Eva were touchy about money, all the stuff they couldn't buy. Sunglasses were their obsession, every few months a new pair.

"Dad feels like a loser because he can't buy a place he actually likes," Nan said.

"Of course he can't," Eva added. "He can't hold a job more than thirty seconds."

A place Dad liked? That meant a place on the ocean if not a houseboat. Dad often stood on the red-rock lawn, blandly returning neighbor howdys, neck muscles taut as he strained for the sea. Jay, meanwhile, was seasick: sick of the sea. He strained in his own direction, following the palm trees straight up, then outward along with the power lines, slashing off to everywhere.

It wasn't always so bad. Jay recalls peeking into the backyard and seeing his dad spray his mom with the garden hose, and her laughing, and their wet, happy, gripping hands. He remembers Nan and Eva playing a game of flicking their ponytails for Dad to try and grab, then squealing when he caught them. Jay played no such games back then, but Nan's and Eva's frivolity brought him hope that one day he might.

Hope collapsed every morning at six a.m.: *Sleepers, arise!* Jay began to see Dad's siren as the opening punch of a boxing match, Mitt Gardiner versus his life. Dad didn't want the house, not really. He didn't want the family, not always. Only Jay, by bad luck the only other balls-haver in the house, was doomed to join Dad's fight, to be brought up as a first mate on a ship headed straight for the rocks.

2974 PSI

Jay can't sprint in full dive gear but takes off as fast as he can.

When diving with a buddy, or one's hard-ass father, there's a checklist. How's your buddy's physical and mental sharpness? How's your own? What's the navigation plan? The depth expectation? Do we know our hand signals? Is air flowing? Are the cylinders secure? Jay alarm-clocked himself before dawn—his own *Sleepers, arise!*—to drill the checklist into his brain and consult local tide tables, so he might enter the water between ebb and flood. On the drive down, he tuned in to the weather, ten-to-fifteen-knot winds, seas three-to-five feet, small-craft advisory, an overall marginal day for diving.

No stopping now. He doesn't even glance at the beach crowd. His left foot smacks into fizzing, iridescent surf, his right leg sinks to the shin, and he's in it, marching through rocks, elbowing aside high spits of salty spray. He swings his mask through a vane of water and the baby shampoo runs, and as he's dodging boulders, he's wiping the faceplate with his thumb, defogged now, ready to roll. Fins tucked under his armpit as he affixes the mask over his eyes and nose, motionless for a single second. Too long: a wave like a chest of drawers bashes him from the left—only on Monastery Beach do waves make blindside attacks.

Jay is hurled but his naked toes dance along a boulder's blade and plant into sand while his right hand lands in perfect starfish shape atop a rock. Using these three limbs, he springs toward Japan, the next wave staving against his chest, blinding him with gray spray and black sickles of kelp.

Velocity wins and he splashes down on his stomach, right hip only briefly bouncing off the ocean floor. Here's the magic, the marvel of lessening, every pound of his BCD and cylinder disintegrated as he's cradled in the sea's saline. Jay's himself again, only himself, nothing pulling, nothing dragging. He rolls to his back, fits his right fin over his right foot. They make pocket fins to attach to diving boots, but that wasn't how Mitt taught him. The closer to naked you are, the better, the safer, the realer.

With one fin he kicks and kicks, belly up, eyes to the beach, where white surf claws the sand before retracting. The water fades from fatigue gray to glass blue: here, right now, Jay feels the galactic suck all the beach signs warned of. The ocean floor drops hard from two feet down to fifteen. The cold phantom hand of the Monastery's danger zone curls around his waist.

Jay's kicks feel like a baby's fussing. He goes nowhere but down.

Did he only survive earlier Monastery dives thanks to the babysitting of the great Mitt Gardiner? Jay has stayed plenty active since leaving home. Basketball with Chet. Jogging with Tekla and Mandy. He bikes damn near everywhere he goes. But a diver's muscles are different, and the skintight Henderson tells him precisely what two years off have cost. Abs like dough, thighs like sticks, lungs that think they know aerobic exercise but really don't.

He paddles harder. He feels the rip current yank.

2013

"What's the difference between a rip current and a riptide?"

"A riptide is . . . It's, like, when a tide pulls water along the beach."

"Especially a place with a jetty, like an inlet. And a rip current?"

"That's where the backwash comes through, like, a break in the sand bar. And zoom!"

"What are a diver's three air pockets?"

"I met a kid named Jetty."

"No you didn't. What's the three air pockets?"

"I did, too. Oh, wait. *Jerry.*"

"Focus, Jay."

"The lungs and the mask and the . . . eucalyptus tube. In your ear."

"Eustachian tube. What do you call the electroreceptors in a shark's skull?"

"The electro . . . Dad! That's too hard!"

"Every guy you see working here, if I asked them, they'd know. You want to be able to talk to them without embarrassing yourself?"

"I *don't* want to talk to them. I want to go home."

"We're not going anywhere till you get these right. Facts are important. The answer is Ampullae of Lorenzini."

"That's a stupid fact! No one knows that fact!"

"Well, now *you* know it. Someday, in some way you can't imagine, one of these so-called stupid facts is going to save your stupid life."

2941 PSI

Mitt taught him what to do. Don't lose your damn head, first of all, then paddle parallel to the beach, a few feet ought to do it, a rip current's channel is narrow, hourglass-shaped. Jay's not going to give Mitt too much credit. Any swimming booklet, any internet search, will tell you the same thing.

Sure enough, a few paddles, and the blistering seethe lets go. Like that, Jay's past the break. He floats, puts on his left fin, breathes hard through his regulator. The splashing is crisp through his hood and feels nice on his hot cheeks. With waves this choppy, he doubts the Dirty CGs noticed him. But he's got some struggle ahead. Rocks aren't the only reason divers don't enter from here.

A thick black shadow runs a thousand feet straight into the bay like a slinking prehistoric serpent. The kelp forest. Underwater, it's a photographer's paradise, stalks reaching forty feet tall, a real mysticism to the undulating green against the water-rippled furnace of sun.

At the surface, the kelp forest has the quality of an oil spill.

Jay aims for what looks like the thinnest patch. A swell lifts him, the kelp vanishes, then the wave rolls on and he's dropped into an open palm of mustard-colored leaves half his size. They slop around Jay's arms and legs like tongues, a heavy, drooling grip. He tries to kick away but only gets both legs swaddled in deeper leaves.

He thrashes, but it's like fighting off wet blankets. Jay's pulse quickens. He doesn't remember the kelp forest ever being this thick. Mitt would have loved it. He was obsessed with the purple sea urchins annihilating the kelp, positive that humans were to blame. Probably true, but it's also humans who invented the BCD, and without it, Jay would be under the kelp already, a place thick, dark, and confusing.

Jay ducks underwater for the first time, a green world, and tears long, gummy blades of kelp from both ankles. Then kicks, kicks, aiming himself between stalks.

He's free. He pops his head into fresh air.

Regulator laughter sounds like robot gasps.

Never dive Monastery alone, Mitt said.

Well, he did it anyway. And the dangers are behind him.

Take that, Mitt.

Take that, every doubter, every underestimator.

Jay squints through a mask stippled by beads of water. There's kelp slime on his wetsuit. Under his nails, too. He shudders. He's always reviled kelp texture. Too much like flesh. He splashes his arms in the water to get rid of it.

In the blur of his pale flesh, he realizes he's forgotten his gloves. Fuck. Shit. He left them in the car trunk. Afraid of the Dirty CGs, he geared up too fast. He flexes his hands. Not too cold yet, but that will change. Too bad. No going back for gloves. He knows one madman, at least, who preferred to dive without them.

2017

Golf ball collection is done by touch, no gloves. The water hazards at Pepper Beach are legendarily vile. Dye keeps them looking good, but fairways are noxious with chemicals and fertilizers that flow into the ponds, mixing with goose crap to make a silky, black pudding. A diver can't see in that.

"Gotta keep your eyes shut down there," Dad says, zipping his red rubber drysuit. "Otherwise you start seeing things."

This is interesting. "What kind of things?"

"Creatures. People. Solar systems. Your brain puts stuff in your eyes."

Jay has horror-movie visions. "Cool."

Dad smiles through the PVC face shield.

"It is. A little. I used to think so when I was young. But distraction like that is deadly."

Jay deflates. He's twelve and can't say anything right. He ought to know Dad's chatter is to distract from the fact that he's fifty-two and trawling through goose shit eight hours a day.

The only decent gig Dad's had in Jay's lifetime was working as a charter-boat dive guide. The clientele wasn't a great match. Tourists with unbent PADI cards, wealthy teens on Daddy's dime, newlyweds looking at each other instead of the safety demonstration. But Mitt Gardiner liked to lecture. And, after all, diving was diving. For ten months, Dad seemed kind of happy.

He got fired for telling customers how 9/11 had been a godsend for baleen whales. The emergency closings of ports had dramatically lowered whales' glucocorticoids, their stress hormones. When a customer told Mitt it was unpatriotic to celebrate September 11 for any reason, Mitt got into it regarding which mammals were more worth saving.

Dad's voice is muffled through the face shield as he quizzes Jay on hazmat protocol. How does Dad not notice the foursome in the golf cart laughing at him? How can he be so attentive to whale glucocorticoids and so inattentive to human ridicule?

Jay looks away from the laughers as Dad lowers himself into shit.

2923 PSI

What Jay first takes as shit in the water is actually a dead sea lion. It bobs twenty feet off, radiating rot. Its kitten face gone skull-like, eyes gobbled, an ageless agony to its golden fangs. White bone gleams through a red hole in its blubbery hide. Good diver practice is not to dwell on what killed it. Jay pictures sharks and killer whales, their caves of stalactite teeth.

He kicks away from the corpse. He's got to be eight hundred feet out. He pulls the collar of his Henderson to let water skim between neoprene and skin, standard temperature regulation. It's goddamn cold, upwelling from the canyon. His shivers push worms of ice water along his body.

Jay kicks long enough to warm his temp. He looks north at what Monastery divers call the washrock, a boulder jutting from white tidewater a quarter mile off the beach. It's the finish line: you align with the washrock, then drop.

These helpful hints are buried in the mental clutter stockpiled by Mitt. What's the significance of 1,080 versus 4,725 feet per second? The speed of sound in air versus the speed of sound in water. What's the weight of air inside an eighty-cubic-foot tank? $0.08 \times 80 = 6.4$. What's the weight density differential between seawater and fresh? $(64 \text{ [sea]} \div 62.4 \text{ [fresh]} - 1) \times 100 = 2.5\%$.

He'd love to flush all of it from his head.

And he will, the second he lays a hand on Mitt's bones.

Jay's backstroke aligns him with the washrock. He stops, drops his legs, fins cycling easily in open water. This may be the last dive of his life, but he can't deny the old spark of excitement, an astronaut about to leave the capsule.

Jay adjusts his mask, the nose pocket snug, the silicone skirt slicked tight to his brow. He takes the regulator from his mouth, voids it, inhales his last taste of natural air. He peers back at dry land. The beach is all but gone, a white zipper sealing the ocean to the hills. He sees the beach's namesake peeking from forest, the Carmelite Monastery of Our Lady and Saint Therese.

He's taken by a hazy longing; it feels like treading water, keeping afloat in life's rips and surges. Mom's big on church, goes every Sunday to the First Presbyterian on El Dorado Street. Last he heard, Nan and Eva—one in Bakersfield, the other in San Jose—both joined churches. Jay used to go with Mom, a surefire way to get out of predawn seafaring. But after Jay fled home, he accepted he was godless, just like his dad. Mitt had robbed that piece of him, too.

Makes him sad. God might have been a handy wrench to carry these last two years. He nearly grabbed hold of that wrench once, right there in the monastery.

2019

Dad's about to drop for a second dive. There's a three-thousand-pound Mola mola down there, how can Jay not want to see that? Jay's fourteen and bored. Dad's hurt look only steels Jay's stubbornness. Hewey stretches his left leg from the kayak and lies that he's cramping up, he'll paddle Jay back to Monastery Beach, have them an energy-bar breakfast. Dad waves them off. Whatever.

It's early, like Dad likes it. Jay watches the cars wend toward the monastery. Hewey notices, motions Jay into his car, and they join the parade. Despite being a Jewish dentist, Hewey knows everything about the Discalced Carmelite nuns. He describes their daily rituals of self-denial and prayer. Does Dad know about this? Dedication, repetition, discipline: those sound like Mitt Gardner values.

Eight a.m. mass is open to the public every day but Thursday. Hewey takes off his safari hat and starts up the long white stairs. Jay panics. They're going in? Mom's church trained him in buttoned shirts, choking ties, stiff loafers. He's wearing sweats.

"It's not like that here," Hewey says. "Come on, you'll see."

Hewey's right. There are people in dress clothes but also kids in shorts, adults in athletic wear. A loose congregation of thirtysome stands, sits, chants in reply to the priest. A call: *Ayekah*. Response: *Hineini*. The rest is indecipherable reverberation. Jay doesn't mind. Compared to the First Presbyterian, this place is a marvel. Ceiling taller than any kelp he's ever seen, braced in the brown stanchions of a pirate ship's hull.

A sermon. Genesis, Eden's forest, don't eat from the Tree of Knowledge.

The specifics are hard to make out in the tripling echoes. Jay disengages, reads the words *NOSTRA CONVERSATIO IN CAELIS EST* over a door. He whispers to Hewey.

"What's that mean?"

Has Hewey known Latin his whole life? He laughs silently. The long gray hairs of his eyebrows wiggle like antennae.

"Our conversation is in heaven," he translates.

"Why's that funny?"

Delighted tears squeeze from Hewey's eyes.

"Lotta conversation in here." He gestures at the door. "But heaven's out there."

2892 PSI

Belly flop like another of God's dropped boulders.
   But regression to gills and fins comes quick.
   Or is it evolution? Were legs a grand mistake?

2873 PSI

Jay dives. A simple thing to say, in theory simple to do, but two feet under, the ocean is inhospitable. Maybe it gave up on Jay when Jay gave up on it. Or maybe, you know, Jay just needs to release air from his BCD. He gives his BPI trigger a long squeeze, deflating his BCD, and feels the yielding of the sea's turned back. Jay gathers the hoses of inflator and instrument console under his left arm and upends, head down, fins up.

Everything's teal. The bouquet of bubbles from his regulator perturbs a school of blue rockfish nibbling plankton off the kelp. Jay pauses to ensure he's breathing clean, inhaling dry cylinder air and exhaling grape-bunch bubbles, then turns from the yellow-and-green kelp canopy, that last glow of sky, and kicks down into the cold.

Visibility is worse than expected. Green murk. He's stupid, stupid. Why didn't he turn back when he heard the weather report? On a sunnier day, vision might be ten times better. Mitt dissents from his jail cell inside Jay's skull: *I'll take overcast any day—too much sun means too much plankton.*

Jay wills the voice to shut up. Mitt's right, as usual. The kelp forest makes a lot of shade, he's just got to get out from under it. Jay dives lower and the cold water finds exposed skin to caress: cheeks, hands, ankles.

An egg-yolk jellyfish. It contracts as flat as a plate, then expands to eyeball roundness, a liquid cascade of cloudlike guts waving hello inside a translucent bag, before hundreds of tendrils straighten and it propels. A dream of a creature. Ironically, the dream grounds Jay, here where he touches no ground. Hewey might have been right. Where else but heaven could a clump of guts live unaided?

Jay sinks. Cool, quiet. White sand shifts as if concealing a stingray. A large, lumpy rock flutters with violet algae. He's at the bottom. Jay arcs his back, riding the inflator, going horizontal, not dipping now but swimming. More than that. Carried along in an invisible palm. A child in trusted arms. A leaf in a calm breeze.

He's flying.

It's wonderful. Isn't it?

Couldn't this place—the water, not the Tarshish house—have been a second home for him, a sanctuary better than any at the Carmelite Monastery?

There's a tiny leak in Jay's mask. Can't be tears. Maybe Mitt hadn't lied when he claimed to be born in the water; maybe birth is a process, not an event. If that's true, Jay was born here, too. But he also died here, at least part of him did.

He beat Dad to it.

2021

"You ever been to one of them water shows? Porpoises? Dolphins?"

Funeral home. No casket. Dad's body never found. Everyone's upset about that. Twenty minutes till the undertaker opens the door. It'll be Mom's friends, a few of Nan's and Eva's, a scattering of Jay's. Dad's only friend was Hewey and he's seated beside Jay, making conversation. Looks like the old man has never dressed up before. A missing button replaced by a safety pin, tie knot the size of an apple, the safari hat. KN95 mask looped around one ear.

"Yeah. Ocean World. Dad wouldn't go."

Not really the truth. Mom had sprung the Ocean World trip as a surprise when Jay was nine. Nan and Eva ecstatic, Jay, too, until he felt Mitt's cold look. They were supposed to go diving. Mitt crossed his arms. So what was it going to be? Diablo Pinnacles with him? Or join up with the girls at the fake ocean? Miserably, Jay murmured *Ocean World*. Dad nodded, disgusted, and left. Jay was sick to his stomach the whole trip.

"Mitt saw himself like one of them dolphins," Hewey said. "Like he'd been trained to do tricks in captivity."

There's this thing tonight, a church thing tomorrow morning, a cemetery thing directly after that. Jay has to show his face to a lot of people who think he treated his dad like crap, who'd like to add their spit to his shoes, even in the funeral home. How would that feel? How would Mom and his sisters react? When not hidden by his Covid mask, he'll need to manufacture the remorseful expression everyone expects. Maybe he really feels it.

What he feels most is exhaustion. His body has been clenched for sixteen years.

"Not sure I'd call my family *captivity*."

"I don't side with Mitt as a rule, son. I'm just saying, once he couldn't get out in the water much . . . he didn't see much point in going on. The inside of a room never held much appeal to him."

They are inside a room. Jay looks at the clock on the wall. Fifteen minutes till showtime. His sisters dolled up in fashionable black, framed photos of Dad looking happier than Jay ever recalls, the undertaker and his satin gestures. It's a dream-lit place and time when Jay might say anything. Like a confessional. He better be quick before the priest is off duty.

"What did he weigh himself down with?" he asks.

Jay's given this a lot of thought. Sailors as savvy as Hewey and Dad don't try to launch a rowboat off Monastery Beach. They had to have departed from a harbor on the other side of the peninsula. That's a whole lot a rowing for a pleasure trip.

It's like Hewey has been waiting for the question.

"Dive weights."

"You saw them?"

Hewey doesn't look wary. If anything, he looks proud. He points three times with agile fingers that used to ply dental picks and saliva ejectors. There on the wall, an ivory cross. There, a harp in stained glass. There, the painting by the window, Jay's pretty sure that's Jesus.

"My religion, your mom's religion, they're all inside out about suicide. It's pretty clear whoever wrote the rules didn't have mesothelioma. Take Jesus over there. He knew what he was doing with that cross. And his rep's still pretty good."

Jay pictures it. Mitt Gardiner, strapped with dive weights, dropping off the edge of the boat. Hewey respectfully turned the other direction. Jay doesn't know shit about Hewey, not really, and suddenly it makes him ashamed.

"Where you from, Hewey?"

Hewey points again. Through the wall. Toward the sea. The old man smiles.

"Did you know *sailors* and *angels* are homophones in Hebrew?"

2844 PSI

Jay hovers over tufted rocks and checks his console: 40 feet, 2844 psi. For the millionth time, he wishes he had a computer on his wrist like every other diver in Monterey. He'd know his dive time, decompression safety stops, and water temp, and have gas-integrated air pressure monitoring, too. But Mitt regarded Jay's desire for a computer as a consumerist pining for a needless gadget.

Want to know your dive time? Wear a watch.

Your safety stops? Three minutes at fifteen feet, what else is there?

Your temp? You're either cold or too cold.

You want your pressure gauge reliant on batteries? Are you nuts?

Jay waggles his fins. Terrain scrolls beneath him. Rocks upon rocks, dumped here eons ago, an artist's palette of pink algae, red sponges, brown moss, orange sea cucumbers, white worms. The pale discs of anemones are like highway lights, nothing but open mouths, oral tentacles fluttering, eternal hunger. A lone tiger-striped fish looks dead till it twists.

Jay floats past it, tries the same trick.

The smallest push of fin, a slight kink in his waist, chest like a ship's bow, and he's skimming with millimeter precision across haphazard topography. His mask passes over a series of fat California flatworms, a thick-knuckled decorator crab coated in green invertebrates, a bright orange hydrocoral. He lets the blades of a laminaria tree tickle his chin. He rolls upside down to pass beneath a white jellyfish, like lacy lingerie tossed into the sea.

If only moving through the surface world was this effortless.

Was this garden of sea cucumbers the last thing Mitt saw? This sparkling carpet of opossum shrimp? This patient white sea slug with orange tips like underwater fire? The bitter bastard might not have lived how or where he wanted, but he made damn sure that wasn't the case when he died.

Jay bites down on his regulator. The teeth grooves no longer a perfect fit. Over the past two years, his jaw has widened. Didn't it have to? He's been navigating a world of hostiles: angry sisters, contemptuous dive bros, pandemic variants. He bites down harder. He'll dig new grooves. This underwater cloudland is a devastation of beauty, and Mitt had no right to poison it.

He's not here to stargaze. He's got a bone bag clipped to his BCD.

Jay pushes downward. Marine snow dapples past—fuzzy sediment like dandelion fluff made of plankton filaments, shells, everything else. Jay waves it aside, emerges into clarity. At compass west, atop a boulder, he sees long hair in slow-motion sashay.

It's a human head.

2020

Jay feels decapitated. It's two in the morning when he gets home. Dad's truck isn't there. Sick psycho is still out on his condemned boat. Jay's shaking from the cold, vibrating from anger, same difference. Unclogs his soaking jeans of keys, goes straight to his room, starts stuffing clothing in a duffel bag. They'll all say his move came out of nowhere, but they'll be wrong. It's been building, building.

Not a minute into it, Mom shows up, daytime clothes matted and hair askew, she's been up all night worrying. She sees Jay's wet clothes and instantly knows what has happened and what he's doing.

"He didn't mean it," she pleads. "When he loses a job, you know how he gets."

Nan and Eva are in college but home for the summer, and they meerkat behind Mom in oversized jerseys and sleep masks. They look annoyed. But they don't know. They've never known. They *like* Dad. And why not? He's never asked anything of them. He laughs at their stories, accepts their jokes, everything is painless and fun.

"Jay, you're freaking out Mom," Nan says.

"You're such a drama queen," Eva says.

Jay zips the duffel. His phone's probably kaput from the swim he just made, but he grabs his charger anyway.

"I'll come back later to get my other stuff. But not while he's here."

He barges past them. He accidentally elbows his mom in the breast. His heart withers like newsprint in fire. He's never felt more male, more destructive, more like Mitt Gardiner. Nan and Eva stumble out of the way, mouths big and appalled. Only Mom chases.

"Where are you going to go? Jay!"

"Faye's."

"I'll talk to him! Baby, I'll talk to your father!"

Jay's no baby. He charges outside. Phone's dead, so he can't call a car. Doesn't matter. Shouldn't take him thirty minutes to get to Faye's at the speed he intends to walk. His sisters' voices have changed, serious and concerned.

"Jay, take a coat!"

"Jay, you want me to drive you?"

He wants neither of these things. He'll walk until he's too cold and then he'll run. He'll get to Faye Kimmerer's house in twenty minutes. He'll throw rocks at her window. He'll be let in. He'll couch surf for just over a year before finding semipermanence with the family of Chloe Tarshish. Then he will sleep. A lot. It's as if the last look Jay took at his father had imparted a final order: Dad's bloodied face looking down over the deck's railing, right above the chipped black lettering of his boat's name.

SLEEP.

2814 PSI

Mitt kept his head shorn to gray scruff; what looks like flowing hair is a clutch of palm kelp. What looks like a moldered face is the kelp's webby wad of roots.

The ocean is like this; it seems to grow human beings asexually.

Clinging to the boulder is a lobed tunicate the size, shape, and color of a human brain. A Pacific sea peach is a dead ringer for a human heart. A red ascidian looks just like a lung. Off San Carlos Beach in Cannery Row, there's the Metridium Fields, dunes of tubular anemones that, at a distance, look like human bones.

What is sand? The entire sea bottom is a cemetery.

Maybe Mitt has no remains left to bag.

Mitt would love that. So Jay sets to disproving the theory. He checks his compass. Holding at seventy-five degrees northwest. If Hewey was right about the coordinates, and he always was, this ought to be where Mitt went down. Jay pumps his BPI so he's slightly negative, his body bouncing softly off the sand. He takes a handful of rock and begins to pull himself along the ocean floor. He tucks the bone bag out of the way behind him, hopefully not for long.

2791 PSI

Hand over hand, Jay crawls. Cloudy, green. *Dirty martini light*, Mitt used to say. Dirty martinis, Dirty CGs, everything dirty to him, even though dirty was how he liked it. Mom kept the house in hotel fettle— daily fresh towels, pillows symmetrical, vases centered—and when Jay pictures Mitt inside it, he sees a man standing in the center of the room with a scolded-dog hunch, afraid to touch anything, waiting it out, all of it.

But beneath Monterey Bay, Mitt was as curious as a monkey. He floated alongside nettles in endless fascination, as if the swirl of their jelly parts held cosmic secrets. He peeked into dark spaces with the coyness of a spying child. The kick of his fins never tired; whatever was beyond the next plankton scrim would make all other troubles feel small.

But Jay's not after enlightenment.

He wants his muddied reputation cleaned.

He needs to know that he made the right choice leaving Mitt.

That he's *better* than Mitt.

That's he's won.

He pulls himself onward, each handhold expelling a puff of silt. Bad for visibility, and it's about to get worse. Ahead is a rockbound bed, a hundred stone teeth cragged between tectonic plates. Layers, slopes, and bridges, all fine places for bones to hide.

Jay crawls to the first dark pocket, the size of a cat bed. He reaches for it but stops. Dread sidles up at shark speed. He's a kindergartener again with a fear of skulls. What if a single swipe through sand reveals two big white rows of teeth he recognizes on sight?

There's also the fact that sea beasts excel in self-defense. Sponges' spicules can cause tetanus. Scorpion fish have toxin-filled spines. Bearded fireworms embed infectious bristles. Anemones, jellyfish, stingrays all sting. If he carried a dive knife, he could sift through the sand without risk. But he never had a knife, much less a holster. Mitt Gardiner disdained dive knives, said divers only wore them to look cool.

Whatever. He'll use his hands. Jay killed wasps for his sisters, once even chased out a bedroom bird. Same thing here. After all, he's doing this dive for them, too.

The sand in the crevice billows like soft deer hide on a clothesline. Maybe Mitt's whole suit of skin is folded in here. Jay's fingers scatter algae into green smoke.

No skull. Nothing. Frustration, inhale; relief, exhale. Jay grips rock, velvet with growth, and pulls himself lower to peer under a stone shelf. No occupant on the bare granite except a yellow-spotted Polycera atra nudibranch, what divers call a *nudie*. Definitely not dead. Jay drags himself onward, a new cranny, another shallow dig, sand balloons rising until the whole place is aswirl and he can't see shit.

The Henderson feels tight. He's panting, that's why. He pumps the BCD trigger, draws to his knees, floats inside a green tornado. Slow and easy breathing. Purr of air in his throat, upbubbles of escape. He checks his glow-in-the-dark console, dim through the murk: 72 feet, 2768 psi. A tenth of the cylinder already empty.

Can a man really vanish down here? Bones and all?

When before, that man was the whole bay, the mountains, everything?

2741 PSI

Jay peers through the copper-green silt and sees a starfish. Five webbed arms glued to a rock at the limit of his vision. Weird instinct: he heads toward it. When he reaches it, he notices another starfish ten feet farther, plump arms hugging a stony ridge. He paddles over and spots two more, trailing west.

He floats. He thinks.

Stars, pointing the way.

Bethlehem stuff. Mom's First Presbyterian. The Carmelite Monastery.

Lines intersecting.

Hewey's coordinates had to be correct. But Mitt's body could have been dragged off by a carnivore. Jay is probably less than a thousand feet from Carmel Canyon's epic drop-off. Divers without specialized gas mixtures don't swim over the canyon. For good reason. Out in the black, you get turned around, there's nothing to touch, no bottom.

But maybe ten or fifteen feet down the canyonside? With sunlight's shimmer still straight above? Should be safe enough. It's where the stars are telling him to go. He cares deeply about this dive, about finding his father, the good it will do. But if he does fail, the follow-the-stars detail might just be magical enough to garner his sisters' forgiveness. He knows for a fact it'll reduce his mother to tears. She will reach out, hold him, and everything will go back to normal. Better than normal. Mitt's dead.

2021

So Dad's got mesothelioma. Sucks for him. For Jay's mom and sisters. Dad will have to get through it without a son, same way Jay got through life without a father. Not a father who valued Jay as anything but an empty bucket for his pointless knowledge.

Jay misses Mom a lot. The feel of her blouses passing by, her radio sing-alongs, the true joy she shows in seeing him every single time she sees him. Anytime Mitt's in the hospital, Jay pictures Mom alone at home, child-sized in front of the big-screen TV, while Jay's living it up inside the Tarshish family fracas.

Makes him feel like a piece of cardboard being bent.

Jay and Mom get together, but always at neutral spaces, where Jay peeks around corners, making sure Mom hasn't dragged along Dad for a sneak-attack reconciliation. In June, Jay's skulking behind the In-N-Out Burger on Del Monte and watches Mom arrive at the outdoor seating with Nan and Eva. All three vaxxed and mask free.

Jay holds back to soak it in. He hasn't seen his sisters since December, before Dad's diagnosis. Nan a working speech pathologist now, Eva interviewing for jobs with a newly minted degree in chemical engineering. Short fresh haircuts, confident airs. They are striking, somehow naked. Takes Jay a second to figure it out.

Neither of them wears sunglasses.

Their hugs are real. He feels their bones and tendons.

Nan cries. "Jay, little Jay."

Eva cries, too. "Our baby brother."

Jay jokes around and collects everyone's orders so he can go inside, rush to the bathroom, sit inside the stall, press his mouth to his elbow, and gasp the sobs back inside. The Tarshishes are comfortable chairs. But those three people waiting outside are the tones of Jay's voice, the organs in Jay's body.

Big smile now. He's back with two trays of food. He hears an echo of what Dad used to say when he came home with a bucket of fish to fry: *Grub, ho!* His favorite sentiment next to *Sleepers, arise!*

But the mood has changed.

Mom's eyes, never concealed, have always been her best quality, gorgeously cowlike, lashes like kelp fronds. She's losing hair a bit at the seam and trying to obscure it; it makes Jay feel protective. He'd do anything for her. Except move back. Just name it.

"He's asking for you, Jay," she says. "You're all he talks about."

2714 PSI

Mitt taught him color loss due to light reflection. Another way of intuiting depth. You lose red at twenty feet, orange at twenty-five, yellow at thirty, green at forty. Jay's in the violet, past sixty feet, past seventy. Same news from his depth gauge but in different colors. He's deep into the orange, red right around the curve.

The starfish keep twinkling even as visibility tapers: nine feet goes to eight feet goes to seven feet. The length of a human body is all Jay can see. What if that's how it's revealed, Mitt's skeleton like a children's song? Thigh bone connected to the hip bone, hip bone connected to the backbone.

Mitt enjoyed pointing out dead things as much as he did the living. Jay found it morbid; Mitt could tell and was exasperated. If a carcass is large enough, Mitt said, it can feed a diverse population.

Translation: Jay might locate his father's remains from a frenzy of festering life.

Jay oscillates his head in search of a telltale bustle. Nothing. Blankets of arctic water swell from canyon depths, tightening his exposed skin. He's near the canyon edge. No screwups. He checks the bone bag. It makes jellyfish billows. The suicide clip pivots and glints.

For the first time, Jay wonders if taking his dad's bones is legal. The Point Lobos region is a marine protected area. You can't take anything, beach or bay, alive or dead. Mitt loved the rule and reveled in citizen enforcement. Mom, in an honest moment, told Jay that Mitt deepened his involvement in pro-environment plots with every job he lost. He dived beneath catamarans of unlicensed fishermen. He shredded nets. He cut lines. Once he punched out a man showing off a chunk of coral he'd taken from Sea Lion Cove. Landed in the pokey for that and, according to him, spent all night bellowing old whaling shanties with drunk-tank bedfellows.

It made Jay proud. It also made Jay feel lost.

Mitt showed similar guardian instincts toward his family: carrying Mom halfway down Junipero Serra Peak after she'd broken her foot, scaring the shit out of a boy who'd gone too far with Nan, lambasting a teacher of Eva's who'd threatened to hold her back a grade.

But Jay? No whaling songs with Jay. No toting toward safety, no intimidation of bullies. Jay was expected to be the same kind of hero as Mitt. Without any acknowledgment that he might end up the same kind of mess, too.

2021

Nan's In-N-Out burger is a prop. She leans over it.

"We just came from him, Jay. You know what he said?"

"This is a setup. I should've known the second I saw your eyeballs."

"*Don't break my heart,*" Eva says. "He's not saying it to *us*."

"How's he saying it to me? I'm not there."

"He's not always clear who's in the room," Mom explains.

"*Don't break my heart,*" Nan repeats. "Over and over."

Jay feels sick. The Double-Double on his plate is roadkill.

"Break *his* heart? You don't know what happened out on that boat!"

"He's told us," Mom says. "Again and again."

"You don't think he's leaving shit out?"

"He's made peace with everything," Eva says. "It's kind of beautiful."

"Except you, baby," Mom says. "All he wants in the world is to see you. I know it's hard. I'll do whatever I can to make it easier on you."

"Fucking coordinated attack is what this is."

"If you weren't so stubborn," Nan snaps, "we wouldn't need to."

"Haven't I done okay on my own? Straight As? All the clubs and groups? I'm president of everything, if you haven't noticed. You watch me get a full ride to Berkeley."

"You're showing off," Eva says. "To make a point."

"Jenna Tarshish says you sleep all the time," Mom says. "The second you get home, and you don't wake up till morning. I'm worried."

"Like I said. I'm busy."

"You're depressed, Jay," Nan sighs. "Are you this dense?"

"Not about Dad. Not about Dad I'm not."

"He's fighting. Fighting so hard. Every day. Only in the hopes that you'll come see him." Mom's crying now. At In-N-Out Burger. Jesus. "Baby, everything in him is broken now. I know it's hard. I know it. But please don't break his heart, too."

2685 PSI

Imagine the flat-earthers are right. Imagine the planet just ends.

No more rocks, no more sand, no bottom to the sea. Jay floats forward as gradually as he can. His buoyancy is good, it's not like he's going to sink.

But it's human nature to fear falling when staring over a cliff.

The Pacific Ocean floor folds vertically like the side of a skyscraper. Rocks cling to the lip like rotted teeth and continue down, but Jay can only make out five feet before it's all erased by darkness. The cliff isn't quite sheer. There's the slightest of slopes.

Just enough to snag on to anything, including bones.

Jay grips a rock at the precipice, hands ice-cold, aching for the gloves in his trunk. Deep breath, deep breath. The dry percolation of inhale, the goofy exhaled bubbles.

He brings his body over the mile-deep chasm.

Jay's a high-wire walker without the wire. He reminds himself it doesn't matter if he loses his bearings, doesn't matter that he failed to keep track of how many kick cycles got him here. If he swims along the canyon edge, he'll hit the kelp forest. Keep the kelp to his left and it'll escort him right back to where he started.

Jay imagines returning to Monastery Beach in front of all those congregated people. Hunched, heaving, wet, worthless, Faber tank full and bone bag empty.

He's got at least an hour of air left. His hands are cold but functional.

He's staying.

With his free hand, Jay checks his console: 95 feet. Anything beyond 130 belongs to technical divers carrying cylinder cocktails of oxygen, nitrogen, hydrogen, helium, and neon. He and his simple air tank can only descend another ten feet. Fifteen tops. He's just got to stay sharp, get out the second he feels his attention stray. This deep, the greatest danger is the hypnotism of nitrogen narcosis.

2014

"I've seen divers take out their regulators and offer them to seals."

Dad's flushing corrosive saltwater from under a hose sleeve. He squats in the driveway. His torn jeans hang low, revealing not only his underwear but the purple scar where, thirty years younger, he'd been stabbed by a sailboat cleat. His shirt's off, art on exhibit. The curled shark on his chest flashing its teeth at a tattoo of a swallow—the traditional symbol of five thousand miles sailed. Covering his whole back, a lofty, four-mast sailing ship slashed by a ten-inch keloid scar. Captain's wheel on his shoulder. Arms sleeved with a nautical star, a hula girl, a lighthouse, a homeward cruiser emblazoned with his wife's name: *ZARA*. Right foot, a rooster; left foot, a pig: an old seaman's superstition to ward off drowning.

HOLD FAST: a pennant between his shoulders, a sailor's plea that their rigging grip stayed true. *OUR FATHER WHO ART IN NATURE* on his stomach: a quote from *Cannery Row*, some kind of middle finger to organized religion.

Dad sweats ink. Garden hose water trails to the street. A mother pushes a stroller through it. A remote-control car operated by two brats crosses the stream. Wouldn't suffer these indignities on a pier.

Jay snorts laughter. He's nine and should know better. But a seal with a regulator!

"Strikes you as funny, does it?" Dad asks.

Jay holds his breath. *Oh no.*

Dad grins.

"I guess it's *kind* of funny," he says.

Dad guffaws, hands on hips, and gazes around, as if to find more amusement. Jay giggles. He's breathless. They're happy. It's happening.

But Dad's sparkling eyes are dulled by the stroller. The remote-control car. Everything. He darkens, then directs that shadow over Jay.

"Nitrogen narcosis is like getting shit-faced in two seconds flat. You don't know what that means yet. Put it this way. You might start reading your gauges backward. You might see a patch of sand you like and stare at it till you die. You might see your grandpa crawling out of a shipwreck. You might get a feeling the guy you're diving with wants to kill you, so maybe you ought to kill him first. Still sound funny?"

Jay looks away. Sunsplash off trailer park roofs. Eyeball pain. A rogue thought.

Maybe I should kill you. Before you kill me.

2659 PSI

Jay pulls himself lower, rock climbing in the wrong direction. He wanted to dive sleek and didn't bring a flashlight, didn't intend for this level of descent. Visibility contracts by the literal inch. He's searching hard, digging through sand. The motions keep his right hand warmer. His left holds on to the rocks, though it's make-believe security. His buoyancy is perfect: he rises slightly on inhale, drops on exhale.

But it's scary. Bottomless black.

Until it's not.

He feels an object in the cliffside rock and pictures the lower knob of a human femur. He grips and pulls. It flies out, tumbling, not bone but shell, a red abalone, the cup so opalescent it refracts itself. That's what Jay thinks until he notices the unleashed swirls of sand are every bit as lustrous.

A light source has appeared behind him.

Some thoughts, cold and rushed.

A Dirty CG has come after him with a lamp.

The sun has burned through clouds, fog, and ocean.

Nitrogen narcosis is making him see things and he's got to get out.

Yes, it's got to be nitrogen narcosis.

How else to explain how the starfish have turned into actual stars?

2636 PSI

Little white lights. Hundreds in shifting orbit. Reflecting off Jay's mask. Off his fingernails. Off his suicide clip. What is it? What isn't it? Jay's blinkless and, shocking at this depth, breathless. Stars churn like ocean tide, spread thin in cosmic dust, iris tight into blinding quasars. Random morphing until Jay notices a cluster moving in sync, stars glommed into nebulas, nebulas peeling off into separate galaxies. Wheels inside wheels.

Right in front of Jay, one wheel of stars flattens into the shape of a lash. A second wheel does the same. A third, a fourth, every star cluster now an interstellar highway.

This is no hallucination, no underwater UFO.

These are the bioluminescent lights of Architeuthis.

The giant squid.

The gruff suck of his regulator reminds Jay that he's alive. He exhales. Bubbles bounce off his face as if the squid data in his brain is pouring out. Millions of giant squid live in the ocean deep. At least that's the theory. Only a few have been caught on camera. Most of what is known about Architeuthis comes from the rare tentacle washed ashore.

Mitt was among those who saw one whole. Jay's heard the story thirty times. A fishing boat docks at the pier where Mitt's doing day labor. He knows the fishers; they beckon. In a plastic crate on deck is what looks like a pool of orange vomit. That's how soft and malleable a giant squid is, how little its corpse resembles the acrobatic goliath in life. The fishers netted it, already dead, twenty miles off Santa Cruz. Cephalopod researchers were en route, in tizzies.

Mitt runs his fingers over the body. His caressing gesture while telling the tale is the gentlest motion Jay's ever seen him make. *Soft as pudding*, he says, and swears the squid flesh glowed at his touch, a final signal, one captain to another.

2609 PSI

Once Jay understands what he's seeing, he sees all of it. A conical mantle the size of Jay's torso. Eight arms, four feet long each and as thick as Jay's wrists, ribboning as freely as eight pours of milk. The squid's two tentacles are twice that length. The stranger the creature, the more detailed Mitt's spiels: Architeuthis's tentacles are capable of stretching thirty feet to lasso prey so the eight arms can begin their python squeeze.

Jay's body squeezes, too, the fright of the meeker.

The mantle inflates with water, twice Jay's breadth.

But Jay's fear fizzles away with his bubbles.

A "diver's peace," Mitt called it, the rush of tranquility after blundering into danger, often a shark, if not a whole school. It's the hardest subaquatic lesson to master. Most creatures flee the pressure waves characteristic of human diving. Often those that don't are interspecies ambassadors, opportunities for true contact, the whole reason you're down here.

Jay has seen up-close a freakish anglerfish, a see-through barreleye, a raft of abnormally curious otters. Mitt didn't believe in underwater photography, claimed it made it impossible to live in the moment. This left Jay unable to convey to friends what he saw—the spectacular. Soon he quit trying. Did any of it really even happen?

This is happening.

And it beats anything Mitt ever saw.

Brick-red in actuality, midnight-blue down here, Architeuthis is thirtysome feet long from mantle fins to tentacle toes. Half a ton of gloppy flesh, floating in place, spreading like oil, its natural lights the glinting eclipses of a thousand moons. As it rotates, an eye rolls into view. The size of a soccer ball, it's the largest eyeball on Earth, a white disc of flame in the ocean black.

Hewey called it "heiliger Schauer," the holy shiver of being caught in a predator's gaze. Said he saw it in dental patients from time to time. Jay liked the phrase, a bratwurst mouthful; he and his buddies used it to reference bullies. Jay feels it now. He isn't shrimp, Architeuthis's food, and that's good.

But that doesn't mean this thing likes him.

2582 PSI

Cylinder against granite cliff, *clang*. Jay cranes his neck, dizzied by alien biology. It makes him feel small, a good thing, part of a diver's peace, but also big, because *he's* here, too, isn't he? Brave enough to meet this monster at the border of worlds.

If Mitt's sermons are to be believed, giant squids generally keep thousands of feet down. Coming this close to the surface means something is wrong. The squid's sick, deranged, dying. Or possibly disturbed by human behavior. Nothing enraged Mitt more. Fishing nets tangling aquatic life. Toxins released by barges. Climate change forcing migration to perilous new habitats.

Jay's fascination is irked by a clouding vision. Faceplate's fogging up. The baby shampoo's not cutting it. Something to do with the depth? Anyway, it's an easy fix. All he has to do is take his mask in both hands, tip it forward off his forehead, let the mask fill with water, then tip the bottom of the mask off his cheeks while exhaling through his nose. This clears the water, wipes the fog. A physics trick Jay never understood no matter how often Mitt explained it.

To do it, though, he's got to let go of the rocks. He's buoyant, but still, it's total abandonment of earthbound security. He thinks of the In-N-Out Burger after he stormed away, his sisters unable to hide their grief without sunglasses. The canyon cold is their tears, anointing his face, hands, ankles. They don't know it, but they're counting on him as much as he's counting on himself.

Jay lets go of the world.

Quickly, the mask trick. For five seconds he sees only the frolic and froth of suctioned water. Survival instinct engages; he scissors his fins. Should lift him vertically, but instead he's bucked by a current. Must be Architeuthis squeezing seawater from its mantle to dart away.

Jay blinks away salty beads. The giant squid's still there. But it's made a sunflower metamorphosis, bioluminescent lights glaring gold, appendages like ropes of fire. Marine snow cyclones. Infinitesimal particles patter against Jay's hood.

Bigger things hit him next: pebbles, shells, leaves, a full fish hard against his mask. He gasps, but the regulator translates it into just another breath. Something is happening. A tsunami. An undersea earthquake.

The abyss speaks.

TAK

Mitt used to rap Jay's tank for attention, a muffled underwater gong.

This is like that, but everywhere and everything.

The current gets stormier. It spins Jay, skids him parallel to the cliff. He's got no control. He skews under one of the squid's long tentacles, all it has to do is flex and Jay will be snagged, a parcel for deep-sea drowning. But the squid looks equally stunned, jelly quivering with every *TAK*, *TAK*, *TAK*, a cannonade Jay receives as a series of blows to his sternum.

His head glances off rock. His hands go to his head on instinct, and he misses his chance to grab hold of the cliff. A new current shoves him farther from it. He's an astronaut cut from his space station. He's way over the canyon's open mouth. Fish pelt him. Beneath deafening *TAK* blasts, he hears their little bones break. He's in trouble, his clumsy head got him in trouble, just like Mitt always—

2020

"You want your stupid head chopped off?"

"I'm sorry!"

"Is that how you want me to come home to your mother? Carrying you up the driveway with a big chunk gone from your head?"

In the water, gripping the gunwale of Hewey's sailboat anchored near Yankee Point Rock. Dad and Jay, regulators out, mouths dry from the dive but still spitting. Some of Dad's spit is blood—undiagnosed mesothelioma. If anything, Jay's thinking Covid-19. From the side deck, Hewey frowns down at the vitriol.

"What'd the boy do?"

"I made a mistake! Jesus!"

"The *boy* hurried through decompression, then nearly stuck his face into the boat propellor!"

"You ever heard of a mistake?" I cry.

"If I hadn't grabbed your ankle . . ."

"Of course you haven't heard of it! You're perfect!"

"Oh, I've made mistakes. At least four of them."

Dad's facial scars tighten with his glare. Count 'em off: Zara, Nan, Eva, and the everyday insult known as his son. Jay doesn't think Dad really means the first three, but the fourth? It's three months before Jay moves out. He's fifteen. Too old to feel heiliger Schauer when he looks at Dad, too old to take this shit much longer.

"I didn't see the boat. All right?"

"You don't *have* to see it. You feel it. A push."

Jay breaks the stare first, looks up at the boat. Hewey grimaces like he does when Mitt's being an asshole, but a *correct* asshole. Jay knows it. He *did* feel the push, *did* know it was strange, yet hurried to surface anyway.

Dad shoves both hands into the water, splashing Jay in the face.

"You feel that, dummy? That's how you know something big is on its way."

2559 PSI

Jay feels it now.
TAK
TAK
TAK

2531 PSI

It is the moon, pale blue, mottled, massive, dream, legend.

Rising.

A ship of gods from primordial tar, yard after yard of wrinkled black bulk, a farce of size displacing the entire ocean. There's an Omega shape in phosphorescent white, and Jay's stupor permits the dull understanding that this crescent is a *mouth*, twenty feet of closed mouth, and this obsidian skyscraper is no surfacing Atlantis. No colliding planet.

It is a living thing.

Mitt, in his foulest of moods, pissed at some landlubber who got the best of him, said human beings were suckers to think they, with their matchstick villages balanced atop bread crusts of dry land, controlled anything at all.

The lords lived below.

Fins tiny, yet still twice the size of Jay. Motionless now but one flap of them, and surely tides would surge all along the western coast. The mere rise of the beast tossed Jay like a twig and will do it again. He needs to swim away as hard as he can.

Before he does, Jay tips forward, looks past his legs into the canyon gloom. Visibility's better here, if blotchy.

Far, far away are the flukes. Jay knows them by heart.

2012

Dad draws flukes in the sand.

Jay thinks. "Humpback?"

"No. Look."

Dad points at the tip of one of the flukes. Not pointy enough.

"Gray?"

"Grays have rounded notches, remember?"

Jay squints.

"It's hard to see in the sand."

Dad frowns. "Look at the trailing edges. Look how straight."

"Oh! It's a bowhead! We saw one of the those."

The silence tells Jay he's wrong. Dad looks at him like a stymied scientist, wondering who this boy is, obviously not the protégé of the diver whose forty-year catalog of dives have made him a California legend. To those who don't have to live with him, anyway.

Jay tries to look studious, but he's panicking. When he panics, he cries. Crying makes Dad mad. Dad erases the sand drawing, his half-gone ring finger not helping, and stands to gaze over Carmel Beach.

The correct answer sizzles like ocean breakers.

"Sperm whale," Dad says.

Jay's confidence, the sand, both scattered.

"But we don't see sperm whales," he says hopefully.

"Sometimes we do. Out on a boat. But they're rare. That's why you have to know your flukes and your blows. If you see a sperm and don't even know it, what's the point?"

Jay's seven years old and already the retort is instinctive.

I have no idea. What is *the point?*

2503 PSI

In all the art Jay's seen, sperm whales are barges of fat. But when the whale before him curls its fluked tail to the side, muscles larger than Jay pull tight, pinching seams through the blubber. It must be the strongest thing that ever lived, matched only by its unexpected grace.

It holds the pose: a comma in a sentence so large only gods can read it.

Mitt saw dozens of sperms over the years, often in clusters, doing fluke-ups, lobtails, spy-hops, pitchpoling, and sideflukes, but mostly blowholing jets of wet air before filling their lungs with enough to last another two hours below. Mitt saw a few breaching, flying out of the ocean and crashing back down like the stompy feet of giant children displacing enough water to fill the Great Lakes.

Mitt voiced no particular longing to encounter a sperm while diving.

But Jay saw it in the bob of his Adam's apple.

The old father of the sea, Mitt called the sperm whale.

Wait until the dive bros hear about this. Jay will outright tell them. There won't be any more spitting on any shoes. They'll want to hear every detail. Jay will tell them, and they'll start to see that he's not Mitt Gardiner's flunky. He's a man of his own.

Jay goes lightweight with glory. It tingles his fingers and toes. Makes him blink, blink, blink. There might be tears in his eyes, but with the seawater in his mask, who can tell?

The sperm's right eye peeks into view fifteen feet down the endless snout. A tiny, irised marble all but lost in the vastness of ebony skin. Jay feels the eye lock with his own. Intelligence, patience, curiosity. Jay's outside his own body. No heiliger Schauer. This is no bully. The whale is a fellow mammal; its gaze has a simian weight.

By acknowledging Jay, it shares that it has a soul.

2018

Every whale-watching outfit in Monterey Bay promised the same. See whales. Smell the brine. Feel the surfacing splash. Commune with their souls in some profound but unspecified way, then visit the harbor's slew of gift shops to buy a sweatshirt with a whale on it, because you probably forgot a sweatshirt. This isn't the Bahamas.

Three years before his death, Dad's broke, all bridges burned, and decides to throw his hat into the ring. He sells everything he's got for a roughed-up, seventy-five-foot, double-decker, 175-capacity, diesel-powered vessel named *Sleep*—doesn't even bother to change her name. She's unfit for civilians, though that fact's hidden by a layer of paint that Jay, accomplice now, helped apply.

Dad pulls favors, scores a dock space on Fisherman's Wharf #1, tourist heaven. From the deck of *Sleep*, Jay smells the pier's restaurants: crab cakes, fried fish, fudge. His feet smart. He's gone to every hotel in Monterey, leaving info cards for Gardiner Whale Watching. They are garish, printed in Used Cars font.

YEAR-ROUND WHALE SIGHTINGS. 3-HOUR TOURS. $4.00 DIS-COUNT COUPON OR CALL AND MENTION THE CODE "WHALE." ASK ABOUT OUR BURIALS AT SEA.

Business is okay at first. With his copper tan, bristly stubble, weaveworld of tattoos, and filigree of scars, Mitt looks like a real-deal salty dog and there's an appeal to that. Customers take pics with him. Do they think that's a grin and not a grimace? Can't they see the time-bomb pulse of his jaw muscles?

"I'd probably get twice the business if I wore an eyepatch," Dad mutters.

He's triple-tasking, steering *Sleep*, trading whale-sighting leads with other boats via shortwave, pressing half a headphone to his ear to listen for whale song via the hydrophone. Hull bucking, engines abuzz, one-fifth the passengers vomiting. Always over the railing and never in the head—it's Jay's job to wave queasy customers away from the forever-busted toilet. That and deliver constant sugary coffee to Dad in his old *SAVE THE WHALES* mug, not a drop spilled, a waiter unrivaled.

Dad eats a sardine, washes it back with coffee. Smirks at the mug's slogan.

"People bought charity crap like this in the seventies. Ten bucks and they got to feel all high and mighty. And the whales were sup-posed to be, what? Grateful? Subject to our beck and call?" He shouts over the engine grind and nods at the passengers. "How'd they put it on their comment cards? Their number one interest?"

"'An authentic experience.'"

"Ha! Yeah. That's what they *say* they want. What they really want is awe, Jay, so bad they'll pay out the wazoo for guys like us to dredge it up. Because their own awe, they sold that shit off. For designer ex-ercise bikes, bigger backyard pools. They're parched for it. *What'll make me feel small again? What'll make me feel like a kid?* I'm asking you, Jay."

"A whale?"

"Bingo. But once I fetch them a whale, what do they do with it?"

Jay hates being on the spot, where's he always wrong.

"They take a picture?"

Dad winks. Jay trembles. Relief. He got one right.

"And what do they do with said pictures?"

Jay stays wary. "Post them online?"

Dad sweeps his coffee mug across the horizon.

"Used to be these waters were where you found *your* awe. *Yours.* Some jellyfish? A nice sunset? The ocean was a private air tank you could breathe from anytime you needed it." He pops another sardine. "Now we find their awe *for* them. We gift wrap it. So their friends can see and feel jealous. End result? None of these bozos have got anything left to breathe. How would you feel, Jay, my boy? Ninety feet deep and realize you'd already emptied your cylinder?"

2482 PSI

Dad's data pumps into Jay's skull; he's heir to it. Sperm whale. Physeter macrocephalus. Sixty tons, the weight of twelve elephants, its block head taking up one-third of its mass and filled with an oil that whalers dubbed *spermaceti*. Even curled like biceps, this male is the size of a warehouse. A hundred feet away, closer than Mitt Gardiner ever dared dream.

The white arcs of its closed mouth and genitals are only the most conspicuous deviations from its charcoal color. Pale squiggles roadmap its wadded skin. These are scars—hieroglyphics that tell the violent saga of this primeval giant. Battles with other bull sperms. Skirmishes with killer whales. Clashes with human debris. Both the whale's flukes are hatcheted, probably from propellors.

For a flash, Jay sees Mitt instead.

The wedge gone from Mitt's left ear—a fishhook.

The white scar across Mitt's chin—a ship engine room fire.

The top half of Mitt's ring finger gone—bitten off by a winch.

The keloid scar down Mitt's back—a narrow escape from a sinking yacht.

Jay hasn't found his dad's remains yet.

Or has he?

2453 PSI

The Architeuthis reacts. Jay has forgotten the giant squid, a preposterous notion prior to the whale's arrival. The kelp-like glissade of the squid's appendages hardens. Eight arms thicken and splay, a show of strength. The two tentacles, each extended to the length of a school bus, lash toward the sperm, withdraw, lash again, so fast it's like there's no water here, only smoke.

The tentacles don't reach the bluff of the whale's head, but they spin Jay's gears into motion. The whale's squiggly scars are one thing. But the interlocking rings all over the whale's head? Those are sucker marks from other squids that fought for their lives.

Mitt told Jay dozens of times. Architeuthis has only one predator.

The sperm whale.

That's why the whale has surfaced from the canyon.

It is hunting the squid.

Montage of memories. Jay on the garage floor, or dock edge, or boat bench, flipping through whatever seafaring book Mitt let him bring, pages as fat and warped as *Cannery Row*. Drawings, woodcuts, linotypes, scrimshaws, and 3D models of the ocean's most storied and unphotographable duel, sperm whale versus giant squid, Leviathan versus Kraken, rock versus scissors. An old whale requiring more surface recovery time might be prone to pursuing squid that strayed skyward.

Artists made clear what each combatant brought to the fight. Whales have the power, the weight. But each squid arm is a glut of suction cups, hundreds, each ringed in serrated teeth capable of sawing through whale flesh. Artwork portrayed lots of thrashing, the whole sea at a boil.

Jay might not survive it.

I need to leave, he thinks.

He kicks for the cliff, stirring the canyon's crypt. His exhaled bubbles occlude his vision: he's barely moving. Arms are of little help when diving, but Jay paddles them enough that his tucked hoses come untucked, the instrument console, backup regulator, inflator trigger, and bone bag expanding like tentacles of his own.

The jagged cliff lurches closer, good, then flashes white from the squid's flaring bioluminescence. Bad. Marine snow streaks by, sucked toward the titans moving behind him; holy fuck, Jay needs to *move*. He stretches for the nearest rock. Gorgeously solid, a fireworks display of coralline algae, frilly sponges, bright tunicates, sparkling Bryozoa, a spangle of snails.

The last starfish Jay saw is still there, welcoming him back to Earth.

Two years is too long between dives: Jay miscalculates his reach. He swipes for a handhold of the cliff and gets nothing but a return wave of starfish tube feet. He tumbles, awkward. His tank weighs nothing underwater, but he feels its mass by how quickly he's facing the world's bottom. It's okay, don't panic, roll over, find the canopy of sun-touched water, go that way.

TAK

This close, it's like being hit with a cannonball.

Jay's flesh ripples, muscles wobble, tendons twang, bones ring.

Eyeballs rattled, he's blind. When sight splotches back, the bay's sunny lid is lost, he's in midnight somersault. Mid-spiral he understands the noise is powerful enough to crack his ribs into his lungs. It's the sonic wallop Mitt used to listen for through *Sleep*'s hydrophone.

The sperm whale's echolocational clicks.

2402 PSI

TAK

It hurts, muscle-deep, organ-deep. Jay needs to triple his efforts. Swim so hard his limbs dislocate. Find a gap between cliff rocks and take cover from the whale's decibels, right alongside Mitt Gardiner's bones, if he's lucky, one last father-and-son adventure beneath the sea.

He never gets a chance.

TAK

In Monterey, they teach whale noises in schools. Those forlorn whale songs they slap on CDs for tourists are moaned by toothless humpbacks. Sperms are the only whales that converse via click codas, a language scientists still can't decode. Nothing made Mitt happier than aquatic creatures baffling humans.

TAK

Language is only the first of echolocation's uses. Muscles in the sperm whale's nose clap together to make a shock wave that bounces off the back of the whale's skull, fires through layers of fat, and lasers into the ocean. Anything the shock wave hits reflects back to the whale, translated into navigational data.

TAK

Sperm whale clicks are the loudest sounds ever made by a living thing. Louder than jet engines. Than underwater bombs. Able to stun squids thirty feet away. Mitt knew a diver who swam alongside a sperm calf and had his hands paralyzed for hours by its clicks. This left no doubt in Mitt's mind. If a sperm whale *wanted* to stun a diver?

Jay can still see Mitt's delighted grin, hear his giddy voice.

It'd break every bone in your body.

2373 PSI

Galaxies whiz overhead, the squid's bioluminescent flesh blurred in motion. Jay thinks Architeuthis is making its escape until he sees all ten appendages streaming the wrong direction. The squid is being pulled through the water. Jay is startled but glad the beast is exiting, until he realizes he's being pulled, too. Frenzied, he looks down at his body. Nothing's touching him.

Jay fights the invisible foe, he tosses, he kicks. The view from his mask is abridged, obscured. Bubbles, his own; an ogling eyeball, the squid's; the burly bow of a fleshy ship, the whale's. The sucking force pulls his tendons, bone-ends eight-balling into sockets. Pure panic whines from Jay's chest. What's happening? Cylinder malfunction? Canyon rip current?

Then Jay's facing the whale, and the oily megalith splits open as if by ghostly hatchet. The bottom jaw lowers six feet. After that, all Jay sees are teeth. Forty, fifty, sixty teeth.

2348 PSI

Mitt emphasized that sperm whale suction was still a theory. Some think whales simply outswim their prey. Some think their echolocation blasts are weapon enough. Many, though, insist sperms feed via suction. Mitt knew a woman who'd helped cut up a dead sperm whale with no bottom jaw, lost in battle or accident. Yet still it had a bellyful of squid. Pretty strong argument for suction, Mitt said.

Jay's a new believer.

The whale's top jaw is toothless, bleach-white gums pitted with holes for sleeving the lower jaw's teeth when not in use. They are definitely in use: a U-shape of chipped, broken, yellow cattle horns as thick as Jay's wrists.

He and the squid are being sucked right into them.

The squid gets there first. The whale's mouth half closes, teeth snagging the tubular mantle and a wreath of tangled arms. Sperm whales don't chew, but their teeth, curved inward, viciously grip. A dark blue miasma billows. Instantly the squid's free appendages fasten to the whale's swollen head, thousands of tiny teeth sawing into blubber.

Jay tumbles toward the whale. He's only a few feet away, no stopping now. The whale is appalling hyperbole, bigger than his house, its mouth an absurdly small chain saw hinged to the underside. Jay brings up his fins to absorb impact.

Head, a landmass—

Jaw, a flaming sword—

Jay hits the whale how he wants, left fin on the lower slope of the nose, right fin on the knobby tip of the lower jaw. But the sperm's head is harder than Monastery Beach rock. Jay's fins are EVA plastic and the left one snaps in half, the blade pinwheeling into blackness. Could have been Jay's foot—his toes, white tapioca beads, are exposed. A rod of pain drills through his left leg, heel to hip, a highway pileup of leg bones. His bare foot slips off the icy nose, souring Jay's balance so that his right heel goes between the whale's front teeth and he slides feetfirst into its mouth on two inches of warm slime, the effluvia of a thousand squids past.

Tooth sockets above him now, rancid black pits. Teeth passing on either side, yellowed cones, one missing, one fractured, one putrid with rot. Jay's inside the mouth. The quaking cave of the mouth. A hangnail compared to the head, just three feet wide. But long, the length of three Jay Gardiners. He bites his regulator, his scream vibrating his skull, and kicks. His bare foot plants into a cold mash. He looks and finds the foot ankle-deep into the squid's mantle.

Clenched in whale teeth, the cephalopod jiggles and clenches. It's losing the fight. Its arms and tentacles flail as if typhoon-tossed, whipping the whale's head with sucker-teeth. Several arms fly past Jay, missing by inches.

Jay retracts his legs. It slides him farther into the mouth.

He flops to his stomach, cylinder striking teeth, tempered steel against relic bone, a tone on the spectrum of echolocational clicks. Teeth are all Jay has to grab on to. He takes one in each hand. Thick as bottles but greased with ocean sludge and squid mucus, he can't hold on, can't hold on, tries to roll out the right side of the mouth, but teeth fence the path, and is the mouth closing? Is it closing? Is that what's happening?

2298 PSI

Whales don't eat people. It's a fact. This sperm is after Architeuthis, probably doesn't know Jay's here. If he gets out, the whale won't pursue him. And out is up. *Up*—the word is an abracadabra. Jay is strapped with modern magic, not only the Faber tank providing the miracle of air, but the Oceanic BCD. Its job is to help him modulate depth. But it's not that different from an emergency airplane vest, is it?

Jay swats for the BCD's power inflator, the plastic trigger at the end of a floating hose. He grabs it, squeezes hard. The BCD inflates. He's swaddled in a puffy layer. He feels an inch or two of positive lift. He's gotta drop weight.

He's never dropped weights in his life. Mitt made good and sure he knew each quick-release pouch ran thirty bucks and each weight another twenty-five, but Jay was drilled in the skill regardless. His hands haven't forgotten.

A gunslinger quick-draw and both five-pound weight pouches fly free. He lets them drop, clinking off a whale tooth on its float down. The D batteries he added for additional weight tumble out, too, and now there's nothing fighting his BCD's positive buoyancy.

Jay Gardiner rises.

His body bumps against the whale's toothless upper jaw. He spins, going belly up, then pushes off from the white gums, mind swirling, *I'm touching a whale, I'm touching a whale,* and then feels his right fin pass through the gap of the whale's front teeth. He's out, he's free, nothing but water, he's kicking, shooting through the blue, oh, Mom, Nan, Eva, Hewey, the dive bros, the story he will tell them—

He's jerked back again.

A slam against the back of his skull, his body against the whale's nose, a hard pop inside him, something broken. What feel like bottle caps grind into his left side, and when he rolls, he finds himself face-to-face with an eggy pile of what look like eyeballs, except hard and sharp as rusty tin. Barnacles.

Humpbacks lug around a half ton of the sticky crustaceans. Far rarer on sperms, but Mitt had a theory on that. Smart sperms— and with the largest brain of any animal in history, sperms have to be smart—use barnacles as brass knuckles in battle with other bull sperms. Jay believes it. Even through his wetsuit neoprene, they hurt like grinding glass.

The barnacles can't be what brought him back to the whale. Jay looks past his single fin and finds the culprit. The bag, *the fucking bone bag*. One of the squid's tentacles has tangled itself in the mesh.

2275 PSI

Jay fumbles for the suicide clip. This one single time in suicide clip history, it holds on like soldered steel. His cold fingers can't manipulate it. Too small, too chintzy. Fifty pounds of high-tech equipment riding on his rib cage and he's going to be killed by this tiny piece of crap that belongs on Chloe Tarshish's schoolbag.

A whirl of motion. Jay looks.

The squid's mantle has constricted to half its size. Deep-sea sleight of hand: it's vanishing. The ten appendages are sucked deep into the whale's mouth.

Architeuthis is being swallowed.

And Architeuthis is gripping Jay.

Jay screams through his regulator, the flood of bubbles his bursting sanity, giving up on the suicide clip's release hinge and just trying to break the fucker at the base. The pale mass of squid arms in his peripheral vision disappears. No, no, no. Jay tears at the bone bag now, trying to shred the mesh. The fat, entangled tentacle goes skinny and taut. No, no, no, no, no.

He is dragged down the incline of the whale's nose and back into the maw. He's staring toward the cliff, he can still make out the rocks, until the view is framed by two closing jaws curtained by dagger teeth. Jay fights, a toddler's tantrum, and gains a yard. His movement is gliding, dreamlike.

A tooth eviscerates the right side of the BCD, no resistance, like it's gelatin. Into dark water confettis vinyl tatters, strips of rubber bladder, and a ballet of blood.

Blood. Did the tooth unzip Jay's torso? Is he gutted?

2246 PSI

Steel-cold water eels through the gash in his Henderson. Like when his zipper busted and Dad made him dive anyway. Air sputters from the BCD, froth in the water, and Jay gets thinner.

That's it, obstruction gone. The pull of the whale's suction is worse than anything in Mortuary Beach's trough. Jay reaches up, lodges a fist into one of the top jaw's sludgy tooth sockets. The suction spins him on that axis. He's still belly down but now facing the throat. Jay sees the squid's tentacles go down like noodles, one dragging the bone bag. The throat's black semicircle rushes at Jay like a train tunnel, too small, he'll never fit—

Jay digs his claws into both sides of the palate, right atop the throat. His fingers sink deep: the tissue squishes, just like the inside of his own cheeks. The slickness is the same, too, and the whale isn't just sitting there, it's torquing, a semitruck making a wide right.

The bone bag pulls hard on the suicide clip; the squid, gone now, still towing him like a stubborn child. Jay digs deeper into membranes with his numb hands. Silky like fish guts, like his sisters' graduation gowns, like his mom's hair. The bone bag lurches away and Jay's chest slides onto a fat tongue, Neptune purple, wide as Jay's shoulders.

Jay's holding, if he can just brace his feet on either side of the throat—

The tongue swells once, hard muscle, a drowsy urging.

It's enough. Jay's hands sloughed off slippery tissue. His body propels.

He's snatched into a black hole, arms, then head, then everything, the whale's throat so lightless Jay's arms vanish in front of him.

Then a rattling hitch: he's caught at the top of the throat, his tank too big to fit.

Still a chance. Don't give up. His mind spins the contents of the half dozen articles he's read about people being gobbled by whales. All of them clickbait: unlucky folks get scooped into the mouths of baleen whales, yes, but a baleen throat is the width of a soup can. Those folks are hurriedly spat. Full swallowing is impossible. Unless you allow for the freak convergence of a diver (a skinny diver) and a sperm whale (an especially large sperm whale), which has an esophagus capable of downing a thirty-foot squid.

Jay grabs but there's nothing to hold inside the throat. Everything wet and quaggy. He extends his right arm deeper and feels something straight ahead. Can't see it in the dark, but it's scooted to the right side of the throat. Some kind of fleshy column. Tapered like a goose-beak. Jay doesn't know what it is, but his survivalist cerebellum feels seawater flowing around *both* sides of the column. Which means he should be able to grab on to it. If he can just thread his arm behind—

The floor beneath him drops away, a mechanism of bone, muscle, and cartilage. The throat vertically stretches. Jay's oxygen tank, jammed before, scoots forward. Jay screeches around his regulator. His right hand slips from the goosebeak. There's a disorienting elevator surge—then forward, hard.

A quick orange glow as the whale skims close to the sunny surface for two seconds, enough for Jay to get one quick, baffling glimpse of a detail at the top of the throat: two white symbols etched into the dark flesh.

Each set like a five-pointed trident.

What kind of whale has symbols drawn inside it?

Like those signs outside Monastery Beach, maybe.

DON'T BE THE NEXT VICTIM!

Then, dark. Then, nothing.

2239 PSI

Behold, a universe.

2022

Emails from Nan: Dad back in the hospital, asking for Jay, *Don't break my heart.* Texts from Eva: Dad home but only because the docs have given up, Jay, *Don't break my heart.* Phone calls from Mom, spasms of desperation, he never gave you any peace, baby, I'm so sorry, but why not be the bigger man and bring *him* peace?

Don't break my heart.

None of these pleas come directly from Dad, never his gravelly hello on a voice mail, no palsied scribble on a letter. The pleas reach Jay as remote reverberations; Jay begins thinking of them as Dad's own echolocation. The dying man's sending out clicks, feeling for who is out there, waiting for clicks in return.

Jay knows he's doing the same. After leaving home last year, he kept in touch with his mom and sisters as often as possible, texting pictures of himself looking carefree, doing extracurriculars, holding A+ papers. Click, click, click. But these efforts waned. The chances of father and son finding each other now?

It's an awfully big ocean.

Mitt Gardiner kills himself on August 10, 2021. Over the next weeks, Mom, Nan, and Eva hug Jay, but it doesn't feel right. Like their arms are on backward, their spines curved the wrong ways. The longer Dad's bones are missing, the more their own bones contort. Jay knows he could have done as they'd asked and visited Dad.

But by the end, Dad's clicks were so soft Jay stopped hearing them.

Eleven months later, Jay can't take his sisters' shaming. He finds Hewey. Not at home, because where the hell does Hewey live? He's at Municipal Wharf #2. Hewey's on his sailboat, safari hat employed, replacing the engine compartment drain plug. He's got a paperback Qur'an in his jacket pocket, replacing his little red New Testament— the New Testicle, he calls it, cutely dangled onto the Hebrew Bible by goofy Christians.

"How's your teeth?" Hewey asks.

It's been a year since Jay saw Hewey at Dad's funeral. The chitchat is nice. Jay has oddly tranquil memories of being in Hewey's dental chair. The ceiling had lights designed to look like white clouds over blue sky, but Jay always imagined he was underwater, staring through clear seas up at heaven.

Hewey used to do the teeth of half the Monterey Bay Aquarium staff. He won them over with biology humor. *If you don't floss, you'll go from a sperm whale to a baleen*—the joke being that baleen whales are toothless. The staff told them all their secrets, which he obediently relayed to Mitt and Jay. They relive a few. Finally, business.

"I want to know where he is."

"The coast guard asked me that, you know."

"You led them off course. Because Dad didn't want to be found."

Hewey sits back, twists his lips, sizes up Jay.

"You know how many minor Judaic prophets show up in the Qur'an? Just one."

"I'm not the coast guard. I'm flesh and blood."

Jay leans forward. His back cracks. His joints hurt. He winces. He feels old. He notices Hewey notice—and it seems to be the sign Hewey's been waiting for. Jay knows he's about to get the goods, the specific coordinates. Only first, a little more bullshitting. With Hewey, that's always the price of admission.

"Let me tell you the lesson of this prophet. *Truth never outweighs mercy.*"

MERCY

2220 PSI

(Where are you)

2219 PSI

((Where are you))

2218 PSI

(((Where are you)))

2217 PSI

(((((WHERE ARE YOU))))

2020

"You know what? I'm glad. I won't be a party to it anymore. The sleazy selling of it: the water, the whales. You understand that's what we've been doing, right? You and me are guilty parties, Jay. Part of the whirlpool."

One anchored boat, sixteen beer cans rollicking down the deck, one father, one son. Jay hears distant laughter, the cluck of berthed boats, flags snapping atop masts. It's a clear night, a billion stars above, and the wharf is a half mile away. But it's windy. Three-foot seas. Even if he screams, he's not sure it will reach people's ears.

Dad's drunker than Jay's ever seen. Nine hours ago, two passengers from Omaha leaned on *Sleep*'s starboard rail to get a photo of a lobtailing humpback and the rail pulled out of the wood. *Sploosh, sploosh*, both customers into the drink, not five feet from the hull, but carrying on with such hysteria that Dad, after he pulled them aboard, yelled at them to shut up. Dad got to taping off the missing rail, but his hands were shaking. He knew his luck was up.

Jay was sickened. He knew it, too.

The call came in at dusk, the hour of the pearl. The Nebraskans had filed complaints. Mitt's license was suspended pending inspection of his vessel. Profits were already shit because of Covid. Now this? *Sleep* would never pass inspection, they both knew it. Dad had sunk everything into this boat and business. Both were finished. So he dropped anchor here and set to draining the ship's cargo of cheap beer, a farewell toast to his final stab at civilized living.

He crushes a can against his tornado brow. There's blood over his right eye. A new scar to join the rest. Blood on his chin, too. Dad coughs up blood all the time these days. Doesn't fit with what Jay knows of Covid-19.

"The more lubbers we take out, the more boats. The more boats, the more nets whales get caught in. The more rotors to chop them up. The more litter for them to eat, whole bellies full of plastic. The more *noise*, Jay, all this sonar, it drives them mad. Then the whales don't shit where they're supposed to. If they don't shit right, they don't fertilize the water for the plankton. Plankton offsets more CO_2 than the fucking rain forests. Then we all die. And who loaded the gun? Me and you—all so some fat-ass cornhuskers could post a selfie."

Another can crushed. Blood over his left eye. Two vertical stripes now, clownish.

"Oughta blow up the boat. Right now. So whoever gets it next can't continue the cycle. I got a basket of oily rags in the engine room. Sky-high, Jay. *Blow. It. Up.*"

Jay's eyeballs are dry, that's how wide they are. He looks again at the wharf, the three-foot swells. He could jump in, swim for it.

"Go ahead, get a good long look at your precious land." Dad's laugh is loud, atonal, manic. Turns into a cough: blood in rubbery strands. "We're not going back. We're going to sit on this deck and drink till we soften into something whales can suck down easy. We owe them that much, don't you think?"

He stomps back across the deck. The rotten deck.

"Respecting an animal isn't gaping at it through museum glass or from the deck of a charter boat. Respecting an animal is *living* with it. The Inuits built their whole society around the whale. A single whale fed a whole village. Every piece of that whale became part of their lives. A tool to use or magic for the shaman—the tuurngaq. Shit. Where's that mug. *SAVE THE WHALES* mug. I want it, Jay, so I can bust it."

Two thick stripes of blood down Dad's cheeks from the beer can crushings, now another down his neck, undiagnosed mesothelioma spit. He paces the taped-off area where the Omaha couple fell. Jay's pressed into the opposite rail, ready to vault it if something happens. In case Dad falls off the boat, too, and Jay has to save his drunk ass. Or Jay decides to swim for shore, an option that feels less insane by the second.

"Inuit whale hunters lived apart from the rest of the group. Went out in canoes. Little bitty canoes. And these weren't unfair fights, they didn't have whale cannons like people came up with later. You fought for that whale. You died for it. Every whale you killed, you got a tattoo. That's how important it was. So important that if you died, they mummified you and brought you on the next hunt anyway."

Dad coughs. Tattoos glossy as if newly inked. Eyes golden as beer in the twilight blue.

"Will you do that for me, Jay? Huh? After we blow up this boat? Drag my dead ass back on a ship? Make a harpoon out of me? They did that, too. I think I'd be happy as a harpoon. No conscience."

Jay stares. There are no right answers.

Maybe it's the tilt of the deck, but Dad comes fast, one second and he's there, looming over Jay, eyes red and bugged, blood mixing on his chin with spittle and beer.

"How old are you now and not a single tattoo? Look, look."

Dad pours beer in his palm, wets two fingers in it. He touches those fingers to his cheek, wipes them sideways. The blood smears in a horizontal line. Does the same on the other side: two cheeks, two crosses. It gives his woozy head new alignment, wild clarity, like his face has been peeled off and pinned to a board.

Dad rips the tab off his beer, brings Jay's hand up by the wrist as you would a child's, and plants the tab into his palm.

"Go on."

Jay stares at the metal tab. Sharp where it was twisted off.

"Go on what?"

Dad gestures at the red cruciform of his face.

"Face-paint, Jay. Alaskan Inuits. Give yourself a little nick."

"You want me to cut myself?"

"Just a little nick. This is what we *do*, Jay."

Jay's fear goes hot, gelatinous, boiled blubber.

"I'm not cutting myself with a beer tab!"

Dad frowns. He reaches into his back pocket and pulls it out like it's nothing: a knife. Not a dive knife, he's not that much of a hypocrite. His eyes remain gold, but his pupils are black holes. He unfolds the pocketknife, then pours beer over the rail.

"That's for the whales. Hunters always make sure the whales drink. Take the knife. Paint your face like I say. Then the whales will know you on sight. They'll respect you. Leave you alone. There's no reason to fear anything down there, Jay. Not sharks, not stingrays, not orcas. Nothing down there wants to eat us."

What happens next happens fast. Maybe the boat bucks while Dad tries to hand him the knife. All Jay knows for sure is that the blade comes at his face. He shouts and turns his shoulder, snakes away, and kicks with both feet, striking Dad in the hip, elbow, shoulder, their most intimate contact since Jay's birth. Dad tries to catch his fall, but his palms crunch down on more beer empties and now he's shouting, too. It blooms into the ugliest coughing Jay's ever seen: blood, mucus, something tissuey.

The boat's not exploding. Dad is.

Jay's up, to the bow, patting himself for wounds, finding none but knowing they exist.

Mitt Gardiner stands, groggy, blinking at his lacerated palms.

His voice is the wind. "What's wrong with you?"

"Stay away from me."

Air from a punched gut: four words Jay's waited fifteen years to say.

Dad stares a moment, then presses his bleeding hands to his bloody face. And laughs. A hawking, gagging noise. He bends with the force of it.

"You're not listening, Jay! These Inuits? Their hunters? That's the life we want. Dry land? The city? Our neighborhood? Our *house*? How can anyone live inside all that *territory*? Out in the water, no one owns anything."

"Then go!"

What a rush to roar it, lungs pounding power.

Dad's on his own trip. He drops to his knees. Presses his palms together hard enough to ooze blood.

"The second you harpooned a whale, you threw yourself to the boat floor. Like so. You prayed to the tuurngaq your line would hold. Come on, Jay. Pray with me. You like to pray, don't you?"

Jay throws a leg over the railing.

And holds.

He feels it. A break in the hellish gales. Right here, this second, a space is carved by the ghosts of old whalers. A space for the reckoning Jay and his father have never had. They can talk. Jay knows they can. They are broken enough at last. Their feud can be grappled with. Understood. Resolved if not reversed. A joint prayer, sure, if you want to see it that way.

Dad glances at Jay, his leg, the railing.

"You won't make it. You got soft lungs."

Soft lungs.

That's it. The open space seals shut.

The swim will hurt, but not as much as staying.

"Just remember," Jay says, "*you're* the one who had a family. *You're* the one who had responsibilities you didn't live up to."

Dad's hands drop. Face paint crosses smudged to gory blotches. Bone-colored eyes gleaming from red ridges and brown burls. His mouth, when he opens it, is three feet wide. Jay lifts the other leg over the rail and jumps, yet fails to evade the last words he'll ever hear from his father.

"Don't sons have responsibilities, too?"

2216 PSI

Gasp: flavor of plastic: the regulator—canned air; swallow, dry: cough—awake, inhale—stench/rotten meat: gag: choke; he slumps, face on softness/softer than water—water; where's the water: he's not underwater: must be on land: somewhere dark—a cave/hole/ car trunk: he's been kidnapped; tries to move: not bound—but it's tight/he's in a bag, a sealed bag; but warm/slick: from blood?—his blood?—and tries to turn over: bags have openings; his tank catches: he's still in diving gear; who would stuff him in a bag with all his diving—

The bag constricts. Hard. Jay's wrung like a wet rag, feet to head, nose bent, mask smashed into his face, regulator shoved to his teeth, the plum taste of a fat lip. His calves, thighs, hips crushed by a metal tenderizer. The bag unclenches, but his rib cage and bones keep singing, he's never been so aware of his internal organs, all those spongy loafs packed together, the elastic scrunch and bruisey release.

Without the metal and plastic of his cylinder and BCD, he would be crushed. Jay should have no thought but rip, kick, escape, but instead, chiming through his mind like a series of bells, is a musical chain of thoughts.

Some animals don't use their teeth to chew.

Some chew with their stomachs.

Peristaltic waves they're called, the same boa constrictor motion used to squeeze food along intestines.

Jay's memory blazes from dim muddle to flamboyant psychedel-ics. It all comes back. Mustard kelp, rainbow algae, tentacled wonder, living mountain, clicks like punches, he's flotsam in the suck, and the flopsy welcome of a lazy purple tongue.

The throat is somewhere behind him.

His whole body is inside the stomach.

2160 PSI

The swallow took two seconds. First, pressure from beyond the gullet—had to be the inflation of the behemoth's lungs. Second, a single, seismic throb—had to be the meat meteor of the behemoth's beating heart. Now Jay's here, six feet farther into the whale, in the black of the stomach, *the stomach*, every fixture of his body sobbing from the peristaltic clench. The space isn't much wider than the esophagus. Jay tries to move but he's sick with fear, all he can do is turn to his side.

His tank makes it difficult. So does the warm, rubbery stomach, which grips like a wet athletic sock. The slosh of seawater against his naked left foot and face. The squelching jelly of krill. The rocky shells of larger crustaceans. Food, all food. He's food, too.

If Mitt hadn't killed himself. If Jay hadn't gone after his bones. If he hadn't swum to the canyon edge. If he hadn't clipped the bone bag to the BCD.

A new spark of fright flares inside his battered husk.

The bone bag. It had been entangled in the—

Cold, wet, quick, and rippling: a squid arm coils around Jay's neck.

2137 PSI

Jay survived ingestion. So did Architeuthis. Twenty suckers ringed in sawblade teeth screw into Jay's neck. He feels his wetsuit hood tighten, then a liquid gush. It's his throat slit, lifeblood slurping out. No, the fluid's too cold—it's the slicing open of his neoprene hood, the compression seal disrupted, saltwater flooding in. Icy liquid slaloms down his torso and exits from the whale-tooth rip in his wetsuit's right side.

Jay pulls away, but where's he going? The stomach stretches, not much, maybe a foot, it's a thick, ropy sleeping bag of muscle.

A second squid arm pythons around Jay's left leg.

A third encircles his waist.

Jay digs at the arm on his neck, soft matter, globular flesh, yet gripping so tight he's got to dig with fingernails, rip through membrane. With his other hand he shoves away razings of sucker teeth, spanking at him, thirsty for the pulse in his wrists.

Wet slaps from all over: the rest of the squid's arms fighting the stomach. Architeuthis is as panicked as Jay, recognizing that its life has winked down to a pinprick. Jay feels the ripple and crunch of another peristaltic wave, but the giant squid, spidered across the space, absorbs the worst of it.

The stomach's gnashing shoves the squid against Jay, the fat, mucky mantle, the gooey pile of limbs, and hiding in the center of all of it, hardness itself: an ironlike beak. Pressed against Jay, the squid abandons its battle against the formless foe of the stomach. All ten appendages curl around Jay.

Strangulation.

Jay can't even gasp. His breathing gear can't work if his ribs won't expand, and the squid crushes like wet cement. Drumming through the squid's jelly are what feel like three hard little fists. Jay knows what they are.

A giant squid has three hearts.

Jay has but one.

Man versus ocean. It's not a fair fight. It never was.

2112 PSI

Vessels pop all across Jay's skin. Bones whine. His throat begins to crumple under the pressure. Then he feels a break in the squid's heft, some part of its biology broken. The stomach wall pressing inward is too much for the squid. There's a cold burst, a squall of cephalopod blood. Convulsions ripple through the squid's limbs, and the barbed suckers go limp.

With a slorp, the slack squid flows upward over Jay's body like a pulled rubber sheet. Jay senses there's still fight in Architeuthis, but a squid needs fresh seawater like Jay needs air, and there's only a kiddie pool of it here. The giant squid is dying fast.

Then it's gone, flushed through a channel past Jay's head.

Fish wash away with it, and shells, and strands of kelp.

Jay's channeled in that direction, too, like toothpaste squeezed along a tube, but he's got the weight of bones, plus his BCD and cylinder. He feels the bone bag's plastic mesh, freed from the squid's grip.

The peristaltic wave settles. The stomach loosens like a relaxed fist.

Jay knows it will tighten again.

Without the wet smacks of the squid, Jay's breath is loud, it scares him how loud, the sterile regulator inhale like the hiss of a bike tire, the exhale like a mesotheliomic cough. In hundreds of dives, he's never heard himself like this. He's hyperventilating. His awareness of it worsens it. He'll run out of air. Well before that, he'll pass out, the stomach will squeeze, and he'll be gone like the squid.

More air, he needs more air. He tips open the bottom of his mask, exposing his nostrils. The unholy stench. Fish market gone bad, brine and blood. The melon sweetness of curdling bacteria. Urine, too, hot, tacky. Could be his own, a soaked wetsuit, but might be ammonia. A memory tells him squids are saturated in the stuff.

He lets the mask snap back. Too late. He gags. He's going to throw up. Please, no. He doesn't want to breathe puke. But taking your regulator out, you just don't do that. He pats along his BCD and finds the auxiliary regulator. He tugs it. It doesn't move. He needs to throw up. He pulls harder. But he's not underwater, so the auxiliary tube isn't free-floating, it's pinned beneath him.

Jay vomits. Gunk splatters from his regulator. Breakfast granola that his stomach has liquified into paste. Now *he's* in a stomach: future paste. God, god, god, god. His lungs feel huge and burn. He needs to breathe. He takes a tiny sip of air, filtering puke with lips and tongue. Then he exhales hard and presses the purge button on the regulator. The rest of the vomit blasts out.

He inhales. His lungs are stabbed by what feel like glass slivers. His own stomach acid. Jay closes his eyes hard, a blacker black, eyelids squishing. Tears of pain ooze through and gum his lashes. Every part of him hurts. There's no way out. No space to turn around and find the esophagus. He wants it all to go away.

Sleep. His only defense. It's what he's done every free hour since leaving home two years ago. On sofas and floors, parks and beaches, benches and bleachers. Why not inside a stomach? It'll make the end come without the screeching fear of anticipation. Jay curls up tight. His whole life, recollected from this spot, passed so fast. Let his death come fast as well.

2083 PSI

(Where are you)

2060 PSI

Gravity presses Jay hard. The whale must be turning. An impenetrable body in flex. Jay's half dreaming. He imagines a submarine with armadillo plates, capable of slinky twists. He feels, or pretends he feels, the echoes of this effort: tractor-sized muscles bulging and locomotive bones pistoning, the resettling of giant organs to allow for this machinery.

((Where are you))

Not dreaming now. Alertness prickling back like a lazing limb.

(((Where are you)))

A question Jay asked while trawling for Mitt's remains. A question Mom, Nan, and Eva will ask after Jay officially goes missing. A question Hewey might ask the next time he's boating these waters, gazing into bladelike waves, recalling two generations of lost Gardiners.

((((WHERE ARE YOU))))

Who asks the question now? The voicer is louder than any canyon echo. It's below, behind, and beyond the deep, a current moving at eternity speed. Jay lets an answer be drawn from his body.

"Alone."

The regulator mangles Jay's reply. But still he prefers his voice to the directionless haunt.

(Open your eyes)

He won't. This is nitrogen narcosis. You don't listen to nitrogen narcosis. Instead, Jay tries to hear through his misfiring neurons. Through the whale. There, behind and below him—

BAUM

—the echoing boom Jay heard while sliding down the gullet. The whale's heart. Then a slushy—

THROOSH

—the whale's pulse, raging rivers of blood shuttling through pipeline arteries.

BAUM, THROOSH

BAUM, THROOSH

((Open your eyes))

(((Open your eyes)))

Jay doesn't want the voice to shout again. Has no energy to fight. Maybe he belongs here. A bit of esoterica rises to mind. In the old days, women's corsets were made of whalebone. Inside the whale's literal bones, he's everything Mitt believed he was. Girlish, useless, a sobbing sissy better off with his mother and sisters.

Jay operates his eyelids. Slow, uneven. Sticky with stomach sludge.

At last the lids pull apart.

And Jay finds that he can *see*.

2037 PSI

First of all, he sees the stomach. An inch from his mask, hugging his fetal form. Pale pink folds bulleted by angry yellow ulcers, jiggling with the whale's sway, a coat of mucus gleaming in eerie neon light. Light? How? Jay searches for the source. It's everywhere. Slopped along the stomach walls. Smeared across his Henderson. It's like the whale itself is weeping light. Fantastical, delusional.

(What do we eat)

The light is a hallucination. So is the voice. Too little oxygen to Jay's brain. Or too much. Synaptic aberrations. Noxious gasses crippling his optical receptors. Or outright derangement, psychotic from shock.

((What do we eat))

"Stop it!"

He's yelling at himself. More proof he's brain-damaged. If not from shock or nitrogen narcosis, from a skull fracture when he crashed into the sperm's nose. What do we eat? What does *who* eat? The whale? If so, the answer is simple.

It eats him! Jay Gardiner!

Easy now. Jay knows that's not true. The swallowing was accidental. Sperms don't want bones in their bellies. They eat cephalopods. Octopus. Cuttlefish. Squids by the hundreds. And squids—

Jay's regulator goes silent. Did it break?

No. He's stopped breathing.

A memory has netted him.

He's a kid visiting cousins in San Bernardino, nabs a rare Southern California firefly, cool, then squashes it and regards the glowy smudge on his fingers, holding back tears. Not so cool, killing this miracle thing for a few seconds of sorcery. *What do we eat?* The sperm whale eats giant squid, the same kind that dazzled Jay with swirls of bioluminescent stars.

Architeuthis died.

But it left behind a gift.

"I'm not crazy."

He's sobbing it.

"I'm not crazy, I'm not crazy."

It's squid residue that lights up the stomach. The few inches of sloshing seawater are lumpy with matter. What looks like junk, trash, dregs of plastic. Most of it, though, looks like weird fish, strange critters, still alive and glowing hazily like lights on the bottom of a pool.

Luminous beings like these could only be found in the Monterey Canyon depths.

1993 PSI

(What are we)

The whale is talking to him.

Nonsense, drivel, delusion, lunacy.

But it wakes up Jay; his brain's a shark, circling. Whales. Sperm whales. What does Jay know about them? Largest skull of any mammal. Doesn't help. Loudest animal alive. Are factoids all you have? Think, Jay. Dad, living room, sofa, sisters, PBS specials. Flensing knives, blubber thick as mattresses. Doesn't help. Think harder. Pinocchio. The Bible. Moby Dick. Whalers hurling harpoons. Hacking open the jumbo head. Draining spermaceti for candles. And machine lube, printing ink, soap, margarine. Tendons for glue. Guts for livestock feed. Bone for piano keys. None of this worth shit. Enough. How long have you been inside this whale? Three minutes? Four?

Stop thinking. Start moving.

Returning to the gullet is Jay's first choice, but there's no turning around. The stomach grips too tightly. Fine. He'll go forward. Can he escape through the anus? No idea, but he can't stay put. He begins turning onto his belly, a real struggle, his tank sticks out too far and so does his right fin. He uses his left toes to rip the fin off his right foot. Both feet, naked, sploosh into stomach muck, all the hidden things. Don't think about it.

Losing the fins helps. Forward, into the darkness where the squid vanished.

(Don't)

Jay drags himself with his elbows, audible squishes.

((Don't))

Why would he listen to the whale that swallowed him? Anywhere is better than here. Jay's nose sinks into spongy flesh. Can't see much. Uses his hands. The texture here is different, tighter, pursing like lips. He fits his hands inside, prayer formation, then pulls them apart: forceps, speculum. The hoop of muscle reacts like a poked insect, retracts from his touch.

(((Don't)))

Jay grapples an elbow into the spasming opening before him, now a second elbow, now he's pulling his head in after, he's through, he's through.

((((DON'T))))

1966 PSI

The trident symbols atop the whale's throat tried to warn him.

He's no longer in the whale.

He's in hell.

Fiery haze warps his vision, it's twice as bright here, so violet it's pink, neon ghosts waltzing over a bubbling, crimson stew, all within a purple-red bag roughly the same size and tightness of the previous space Jay was in. It's sweaty hot. Stinks of spoiling meat. Loud, too: flatulent cracks between the spit, gurgle, squeal, and suck.

Jay pulls himself through the fleshy portal. He's on his belly, water to his chin. No, not water, a sloshing basin of jelly pitted with hard objects. He gasps, instinct, but it's okay, his regulator's working. He screws his legs under him and pushes head and shoulders from the chunky magma. Face mask strewn with globby viscera. Warm, slippery gunk worms inside his BCD.

The voice rivals the *TAK*, a skronk like the denting of a battleship hull.

(((((GO BACK))))

Two years Jay's been on his own. No more following orders. He writhes forward. The other end of the bag is right there, he wants to touch it, but when he tries to lift his arm, it's weighed down. He tries harder. His arm bubbles up from the sloppy simmer, draped in the red hood of a squid mantle, half-dissolved by acid. A giant eyeball ogles Jay as it liquifies.

((((GO BACK))))

This is no intestine, no liver, no random cavity.

Sperm whales have four stomachs. Jay remembers now. Just like cows, goats, deer, giraffe. The purpose of multichambered stomachs is to sort out densities, the softer stuff shuttled off to the next chamber, the tougher stuff staying put for further digestion.

Jay's in the second chamber of the stomach.

Bewilderment turns to revulsion. Turns to panic. He's in a swamp of melting squid. Some are still alive, limbs jerking, flesh bubbling. Jay flaps his arm until the mantle flesh slops off. Hard to see in the leaping light storm but his hand looks hot-pink. Burned. Now he notices heat at his other exposed points: his other hand, his feet, his neck, his right side.

He's going to be cooked alive.

1933 PSI

((((GO BACK))))

The whale's right. But how? If anything, the second chamber's tighter than the first. Maybe the third chamber is better? No choice but to keep going, escape this acid bath before his skin flays and muscles blister. But the chamber revolts, chomps down. Squid goo shoots past him. It's not as forceful as chamber one. That's something. With his elbows, he drags himself through pink sludge thick as caramel, the top of his tank distending the stomach.

There are sharp things in the goo. Makes no sense. But nothing does. Keep going. Jay slides a knee, plants a hand, slides the other knee, plants a—

Pain—lancing pain—

Jay bleats through his regulator. Under the slime, his right hand hurts, it hurts! Jay makes an all-fours lurch, collapsing against the end of the chamber, opposite to where he entered. Gasping, he pulls his right hand to the surface in a splash of pale protoplasm.

A dark orb is stuck to his palm.

Slightly bigger than a ping-pong ball. And, Jay realizes, not a ball at all but an abstract sculpture, brown as polished walnut, a fusion of smooth, curved plates that scythe down into opposite pincers. The top of which is embedded in his palm. Jay's blood, orangish in hell's light, dribbles from the point of impalement.

He knows what this object is.

A giant squid beak. The one part of a squid that sperm whales can't digest. Any Monterey wharf rat, even reluctant ones like Jay, knows the legend, set in Russia in the far-fetched year of 1972: twenty-eight thousand squid beaks found inside a single sperm. More common are a few thousand.

That's the sharp gravel beneath the chamber's slime.

So many things died here. Are still dying.

Jay doesn't want to be one of them.

The beak resembles that of a large parrot. Its mandibles are held together by a clump of beige muscle, acid-eaten and drizzled like pumpkin guts. Jay grips the mandible dug into his palm. It's the hardest thing he's touched during this soft nightmare.

Jay pulls on the beak.

His palm skin tents outward. Jay feels the point of the beak grind against a hand bone. Blood, thicker and darker, syrups out. The pain is polychromatic, barbed wire through every nerve, white blindness.

He lets go of the beak. He can't handle this now. He'll faint. If he faints, he'll die.

It hurts to leave it there, but pain sirens are bawling in too many directions to prioritize any one. Jay's exposed skin is on a slow burn, getting worse by the second. With the beak still pinned to his right palm, Jay leans against a knot of pinched muscle, the gateway to chamber three.

1904 PSI

The sphincter Jay inspects by flickering acid light is maybe the width of his arm. He has a wild idea: stick only his head into it, protect his face and brain. Seconds later, the idea is trashed, as the second chamber clenches and liquified squid sluices past Jay through the sphincter, and Jay sees that the third chamber isn't another bag like the first two chambers. Instead, he sees a narrow tube banking off into darkness.

He grabs it, careful of the squid beak, then not careful, pulling the sphincter, stretching it.

There's no hope. It's too small.

There's no way through.

No way out.

He's fought so hard.

But there's no more use.

Things happen in Jay's throat and head. A feeling dimly recalled: the desire to cry. He hasn't for so many years. No point starting now: it's hard enough to breathe in here. The gaspy huffs of the regulator only make it worse. But none of that matters anymore, does it?

Jay lets his weight slump. He curls up as much as the stomach's shape allows, head and hands above acid. All he ever wanted was to get away from the ocean. Yet this is how it ends. In a stomach that will carry him deeper into the Pacific than any human has ever gone. By then, his body will be molten and he'll flow through this tube, easy, and into the third chamber, the fourth.

He finds breath enough to whisper.

"Bye, Mom. I love you. Nan, Eva, I love you."

The chamber contracts. Jay tells himself it's his mom and sisters hugging him goodbye.

He fumbles for his regulator, pulls it from his mouth.

Takes an open-mouthed inhale for the first time since the beach.

(Put it back)

Thick, moist, foul. Not air. Some toxic gas. Hitches down his throat like a wet washrag. At the other end of the chamber, a fresh squid squeezes in, looks like a mop head, pallid and soggy. Its entry kicks up a wave, Monastery Beach in miniature.

((Put it back))

Burning sludge licks Jay's chin. Spatters scald his throat, he's gagging, he's coughing, he's telling himself to let it happen, get it over with.

(((Put it back)))

Inhale. Pinwheel vision. Inhale. Hummingbird heart. Inhale. Black sponge, self-erase, fade out.

((((PUT IT BACK JAY))))

Brain bad. Not think good.

Did whale—did whale say his name?

1879 PSI

(It is difficult)

"Shh."

(To be heard)

"Shh, please."

(To raise a single voice)

Jay covers his ears with a curled arm, but it does no good.

(Above so many)

"Be quiet. Be quiet."

(Of the dead)

Jay's vision slips sideways. Needs a focal target. He lifts his hands. Magenta. Acid-frothed. Right palm embedded with a squid beak. New lifelines, or deathlines, trenched from barnacles, whale teeth, squid suckers. No telling the damage he's taken where his BCD is punctured.

He only knows one man with more scars.

Perhaps it's due to his sudden resemblance to Mitt that Jay's able to recognize, even inside the whale's rich clangor, his dad's mumbly gnarl.

The voice he hears isn't the whale. At least not only the whale.

It's his father.

Either that or Jay's lost his mind.

What difference does it make?

1852 PSI

(Your eyes)
   (Your heart)
   (Your lungs)
   "Not . . . yours. Go . . . away."
   (Failing)
   "*You* failed. Not . . . me. Let me . . . be."
   (Weak)
   "You're the one who . . . *you're* weak."
   (Eyes and heart and lungs failing)
   (Growing weaker)
   (Remember Jay)
   "I don't want to . . . remember."
   (Weaker)
   (And weaker)
   ((Remember Jay))
   "Shut up."
   (((Remember the bad air)))
   "Shut . . ."
   ((((JAY REMEMBER THE BAD AIR))))

2015

"Bad air down there," Mr. Sheol says.

Sheol Landfill, outskirts of Salinas. Jay's with Dad but excited for once to be along. He's ten. Landfills, junkyards, car salvage lots, all nirvanas of adventure. Bulldozers flatten long ridges of trash, garbage gulls abscond with pizza boxes, dirty diapers, rejected teddy bears. All the good stuff will be gone if Jay doesn't get scavenging!

But Dad's all business. It's two years before the job at Pepper Hills Golf Links, but Dad's dressed in a similar environment suit. No cylinder, though. He's only going a few feet down. According to him, Sheol Landfill has been burying crap for decades, and now a segment of land the size of a tennis court has cratered. What Jay sees is a gray lagoon pearlescent with oils and lards. While trying to level the crater, an expensive drill bit got lost down there. Or something. Jay's not really listening.

Dad takes a breath, dips under, rises. Dips, rises. Dips. Doesn't rise.

Mr. Sheol and Jay stand together. Dozers chuckle. Gulls scream.

"You look like you want to go exploring," Mr. Sheol says.

Jay shrugs.

"Go ahead. Thar's gold in them thar hills. Yours if you find it."

Jay doesn't like the shape of Mr. Sheol's grin. He doesn't want to scramble through the junk anymore. He wants to leave. He wants Dad to surface. Dad doesn't surface. Jay glances at Mr. Sheol. The grin even sharper. Dad still doesn't surface. Jay's breakfast whips thick. He's sweaty. Mr. Sheol sounds like he has an eternity to wait.

"Don't worry. This here's my temple. Nothing happens without my say-so."

Dad ought to explode upward, ought to screech for air. Instead, he peeps his mask from the mire like a frog. Only then does he gradually emerge. He doesn't have the drill bit. He's slicked with brown gunk. He's staring at the sun. He collapses on the trashy bank.

Jay sprints over, turns Dad on his side, wipes the slime off his face. "Dad!"

"I . . . went . . . the wrong . . ."

"Breathe! Dad!"

"Need to . . . go back . . ."

"You're not going back! Breathe!"

Cold heat: Mr. Sheol's shadow. The man chuckles. Doesn't even sound like a man.

"Told you, fellow. Bad air down there."

1823 PSI

Methane.

Colorless. Odorless. It's what poisoned Mitt Gardiner at Sheol Landfill. What turned four feet of scummy water into a labyrinth Mitt had no interest in escaping.

What Mitt told Jay, weakly, on the drive home from the landfill, after telling Mr. Sheol to go fuck himself: methane, CH_4, some real hazardous shit, the ultimate planet-warmer, doubled in Earth's atmosphere thanks to greenhouse atrocities. Occurs organically, too. Natural gas, wetlands, cow crap.

Hell, whale stomachs are full of it.

Methane is filling Jay's lungs right now.

He recognizes the feeling from Sheol Landfill. Simply kneeling beside Mitt at the lagoon, Jay got dizzy, euphoric. Here in the second chamber of the stomach, he'll soon deplete of any self-protective instinct. He'll slip into fatigue, then coma. He'll slump beneath the acids. They will glug down his open throat, start dissolving his innards.

(((((MOVE))))

Jay hasn't followed a Mitt Gardiner order in two years, but he follows this one. The way Mitt looked in that landfill, eyes rolled white, lips rubbery as a fish. Jay can't let that happen. There are better ways to die, even in this stinking, constricted purgatory.

(((((MOVE))))

He plugs the regulator into his mouth. Voids it of glop.

Breathes deep. That familiar dry tank air.

Clarity knives into his brain.

How to get out. How to get out. Jay doesn't have the dexterity to crawl backward, not inside this bubbling gel. He's got to turn around, get back to the first chamber. Seems impossible. But he has to try.

First he's got to get small. He curls up. Neck, arms, okay, but his legs are being sluggish. What if they're melted already, cheesy flesh dangling off white bone? His sinks a hand under the boiling bile, finds his thighs, manhandles one knee to his chest, then the other. He's sitting upright. Okay. Good. Now, tuck and roll forward, a gymnast in slow-motion dismount. His hooded scalp scrapes along the top of the stomach, stretching it just enough for his head to pass. The valve of his tank snags muscle, but Jay's got gravity on his side. The tank skids across mucus and he flops forward, splashes down, head under acid. What will happen to his face? Fuck it. Faces aren't a worry when the body you're inside isn't yours.

He's done it. He's turned back around, facing the first chamber again.

((((MOVE))))

Jay's hands, even the beaked one, tighten his BCD. Doesn't even think about it.

This is how well he was trained.

1774 PSI

Jay's had enough stomach viruses to know that bodily systems revolt, and when they do, it doesn't matter if a digestive tract was designed as a one-way street. Wrestling through the second chamber's pulp is like digging through scorching clay, until he reaches the loosened sphincter and clambers through, home sweet home, this time feet toward tail, head toward head.

The whale, Jay's universe, changes direction, and Jay, puny moon, orbits within.

He's flat, stomach down, and bounced in the membrane sling. His lungs aren't lungs, they're puffed, throbbing bruises. He heaves, regulator clicking and hissing like a gas stove refusing to light, he can't get enough air, not even close, and his tank is a thousand pounds on his back. His head feels airy. Between gasps, words.

"I can't—"

(Breathe)

"I—know!"

(Breathe)

"I know—that!"

(Breathe)

"You think—I don't—know?!"

If he could see, fixate on something, it might help. But it's dark compared to the acid pit. No, it's just plain *dark*. He has a stray thought of crusty old whalers of the 1800s, draining spermaceti oil for candles. If Jay could drill upward to the spermaceti now, find a way to light it. It'd be like that video he saw of the gas pipeline fire in the Gulf of Mexico.

He'd be an underwater fountain of flame. A beacon.

But all he's got to see by are splotches of squid residue and a few glowing floaties inside the seawater spill. It's like light leaking beneath a closed closet door. Jay tries to embrace the comparison. He's a little boy and closets are scary fun, all new novelties of black.

The stomach contracts.

The whale knows he's back.

It's worse without the buffer of the giant squid. The Faber tank is driven into Jay's vertebrae. He thinks he hears the dolphin whine of bending steel. Every ball of bone in his skeleton—shoulder knobs, elbows, hips, knees, ankles—are fastballs against brick, nerve endings pinned. Hard parts of the BCD imprint deep into his flesh.

One upside: he barely feels the itch of his acid burns.

The squeeze subsides. But the stomach is tireless, it can do this all day. Jay won't survive the next few minutes if he can't brace against the pressure. He digs his fingers into the stomach walls, wet membrane, and pushes out, but the stomach doesn't give enough for him to straighten his arms and lock his elbows.

(Everything you)

"Shut . . . up."

(Everything you need)

"Shut . . . *up*."

(Everything you need you brought with you)

What does that even mean? It's folksy junk Mom might cross-stitch. *Bloom Where You're Planted. When Life Shuts a Door, God Opens a Window.* What did Jay bring with him that's so indispensable? A go-getter attitude instilled in him by dear old Dad? A vat of knowledge only the lucky son of the great Mitt Gardiner would have access to?

It's typical Mitt bullshit. Riddling gibberish. Ace the pop quiz or we start from the top.

"I brought . . . nothing. You gave me . . . nothing."

(Reach out)

"What . . . ? Why would I—"

(Reach out)

"When did *you* ever—"

((((REACH OUT))))

Jay does it, because Mitt might still be learning to speak whale, and struggling with the technology as he often did. Jay reaches out and feels plastic. In this indecent fantasia of flesh, it feels solid and familiar, and Jay hugs it to his face.

He brought something with him after all.

1745 PSI

Jay pictures it: his left fin striking the sperm whale's alpine nose, snapping in half, tumbling into the void. But his right fin stayed on until he toed it off to ease passage into the second chamber. Here it is, right where he left it. It feels nearly organic, the closest science has come to creating artificial flesh. The EVA plastic is both stiff and flexible.

Like the stomach itself.

Jay lodges the fin's heel into the stomach beside his head. He hinges the blade upward. It's too long to stand upright, but that's the point: Jay bends the blade sixty degrees to wedge it into place. Tricky with the squid beak stuck to his right palm, but he pulls it off. The stomach ripples, unhappy, and clenches down. But the fin acts like a tent pole and the powerful, gripping muscles enact less than half their previous strength.

Victory electrifies Jay's body.

"Ha! Ha!"

He collapses. Diaphragm quivering. Ribs ringing. Regulator hissing.

"Take that! Take that, whale!"

Hissing.

Jay's victory fades.

It's the sound of his gasped air. He's never breathed so much of it so fast.

What's his tank pressure?

How much more air does he have?

Jay runs a hand down his side until he finds the hose leading to the instrument console. It's pinched under his pelvis, and yanking it out is like tugging his own intestines. The console snags on stomachs: the wetsuit's, the whale's. The hard plastic plows a bruising trail up his chest and neck.

It pops free, a bright surprise. The two dial faces are glow-in-the-dark limes. The compass says he's headed north. Does a compass work inside a whale? The depth gauge says 100 feet, but same question. The pressure gauge, though, there's no reason it shouldn't be accurate. Jay holds it flat to his mask.

1720 PSI

1720 psi. That's not good.

Jay's been inside the whale twenty minutes, twenty-five max, and in the ocean another twenty before that. Mitt taught him consumption-rate formulas, a fiddlier calculus than anything taught at school. SAC rate, RMV rate, tank conversion factor, depth factor, multiply this, divide that, with the final quotient being How Long Your Air Will Last. More reliable than all that, though, is Jay's mental log of past Monastery Beach dives. He's been using his tank for fortysome minutes. His SPG shouldn't be this low.

He's guzzling air.

Jay pictures the Faber on his back: silver, chipped, pinged with dents, but solid. Elkhorn Dive Center filled it to 3000 psi. He should get ninety minutes from it, easy. The fact that he's skinny might buy him another five or ten. He's not sure, he's never been dumb enough to push it. When a diver's tank hits 500 psi, a diver surfaces. Rules even Mitt played by.

Fear's quills press at Jay's jugular. All those numbers are crap if he keeps gorging. The tank will be spitting dust in a half hour. He's got to slow his breathing. Slow it way down. He's got to think of everything

(Everything you need)

that might help him.

(You brought with you)

But how? How when he's so shaken? When he's one small heart against nature's scalpel.

Doesn't matter how many dives Jay's done. His instinct is to hold his breath as long as possible, carve out a slice of air he can enjoy later. But the first rule of the first certification course he took was *don't hold your breath*. Let's say you're diving, the instructor said, let's say fifty feet down, fit as a fiddle, but what you don't know is that a big wave is passing overhead and you're actually at *sixty* feet, and that's the moment you decide to hold your breath, and boom, one second later the wave's passed and you're back at fifty. A ten-foot change, that fast, is rolling the dice of lethal disorders.

Gas embolism. The bends. Seizure, heart attack, blood clots.

The rest of the aspiring divers were older than Jay, but he wondered if they were thinking what he was thinking. How vulnerable they were in the ocean despite the tech buckled to their bodies. Humans might have come from primordial waters, but they had made their choice of dry land.

1693 PSI

A sudden ten-foot change on the surface is nothing next to what a sperm whale can do. Sperms dive straight down to echolocate prey, stun them, and slurp them in the abyssal dark. If this whale does anything like that, Jay will implode from the pressure. So, no, holding his breath isn't an option. But simply lying here, his pressure gauge has fallen another 27 psi. His bruised lungs are in a frenzy. He's gasping.

(Breathe)

"Don't—start."

((Breathe))

"What do you think I'm—"

(((Breathe)))

"I don't need you to tell me—"

(((Breathe sleepy)))

Jay shuts up.

It's been a long time since he's heard that phrase.

2014

Jay's nine. Back when he still obeyed shouted commands. He's inside another stomach. At least it feels like it, strapped tight under bedsheets that wick up his tears. A stomach within a stomach: his tummy burns with anxiety. Bedsprings shaking because he can't stop crying, crying, crying. He's doing terribly in school. He thought he could hide it, but there was a meeting. He's going to flunk. He's going to be held back from the rest of his class. He's going to have no friends for the rest of his life.

Mom's already been in, pet his head, told him it's all going to be okay. But the crying's out of control. He's having trouble breathing. He might throw up, pass out.

The door clicks open. Dad's outline carves the hallway light. Tattoos and scars invisible.

"Your mother asked me to come in."

Jay knows how he looks. How he sounds. Gasping. Whimpering. Wet, girlish, detestable. Dad's shame must exceed Jay's own.

"Listen, all this stuff. Math, social studies, whatever. You succeed, you fail—once you grow up, none of it matters, all right? You're little and don't get it. But trust me. Nothing looks so bad the next day. You just gotta stop crying, Jay. It's upsetting your mother."

No, it's upsetting Dad. Jay's loud, hiccupping, hitching chest keeps the tears pumping onto his cheeks, caustic with salt. He wishes Dad would kill him. A quick flash of knife, better for them both.

"Go to sleep, Jay. Please."

Awkward, nervous, Dad sits on the edge of Jay's bed. Eyes obsidian glints. Smells like his tattoos. Jay sobs, chokes, coughs, wails. Dad's woken up Jay so often: *Sleepers, arise!* But not once has he put him to sleep. He'll fail. Dad doesn't know how it's done, all he knows is how to order Jay around.

What Dad says is a surprise.

"You're hyperventilating. It's something I know about. Any diver who's paid their dues has hyperventilated. Big clouds of bubbles in the water, you can tell right away. So I'm going to help you out, okay? Can you listen?"

Jay looks through a gel of wobbling tears, nods his head, the tears falling.

"It's the same stuff we've talked about with diving tanks. You're breathing out more CO_2 than you're breathing in oxygen, which makes your brain go goofy. Your thoughts are flying all over the place, right?"

It's true. Jay nods. More tears spill.

"Put your lips like this. Like you're whistling. There we go. Now breathe into your diaphragm, not your lungs. I want to see that belly pooch. Good. Give me five more. Now hold your breath. Ten seconds. Can you do that? Three, four, five, six, seven, eight—now let it out. Back to the diaphragm, give me six breaths. Now let go. Don't think about it. See? We call this *breathing sleepy*. The best way to dive, nice and slow and deep. Your head's feeling less goofy now, right?"

Dad's right. The tight red bands hog-tying Jay are loosening. He's seeing things besides a black, blotched future. He's feeling the bed again, the floor, the house, all solid objects. Mostly, to his incredulity, he's seeing Dad, right there, six inches away. Dad's not visibly repelled. He's even smiling. Almost proudly? Proud of him? The sobbing brat?

The look Dad's giving him, he's given it before. Jay's only forgotten it. The first time Jay flushed his BCD air cell without being asked. When he spotted a distant waterspout before Dad or Hewey. Non-diving scenarios, too. Jay hitting the ball in Little League, taking shots at the doctor's office like a champ.

Maybe Dad's pride has always been there.

Maybe Jay needs to slow his furious breath to see it.

1641 PSI

(Listen)

BAUM, THROOSH

The whale's heart and

(Your heart)

BAUM, THROOSH

the whale's lungs.

(Your lungs)

BAUM, THROOSH

all working in slow-motion symphony.

BAUM, THROOSH

Breathe sleepy. Breathe sleepy.

BAUM

Jay times his breathing to the whale's biology. He inhales with the heart's thunder, and then, because the whale's life systems operate at a glacial pace, he waits until

THROOSH

to let the air out. And again. Heart, sleepy, pulse, sleepy. The whale is guiding him. All Jay has to do is follow. Feel it now, the untying of fevered knots. He won't achieve Mitt's fabled diver's peace, but if he keeps it up, he might earn an extra fifteen minutes of air. New space opens in the whale's stomach. Not physical. Mental. A space to plan. To think. To see. To hear. To touch. To taste.

To smell.

1618 PSI

Blood. He smells blood. Not the cellophane broth of fish, but a meatier mammal funk.

It's too dark to see if the stomach seawater has clouded red. Jay squirms his hand along his side and explores the gash in his BCD. Doesn't feel a puncture in the flesh, though his fingers are acid-burned and maybe no good. With his other hand, he pokes at the left side of his neck, where squid's rotary suckers mangled his hood—

The flesh there is shaved like coconut.

"Oh no."

Even scorched fingertips can differentiate the outer layer of skin from its spongier underlayer. Jay saw this layer after wiping out on Chloe's skateboard last year and snapping back a toenail. Jay grimaces and probes deeper. A looser, cheesy substance. Some kind of fat? At the deepest point of the wound, a well of hot, bubbling blood.

Adrenaline must have hidden the pain this long.

Breathe sleepy. Breathe sleepy.

But he's bleeding out! He has been all along!

None of his vertigo has been due to nitrogen narcosis or head trauma.

He won't survive long enough to escape if he doesn't stanch this wound. Jay faces his console at the stomach's half foot of slush. There's a hodgepodge of swallowed junk in the stomach. Maybe there's something useful. He paws through cold krill and slaps aside a snapping crab. He finds objects and holds them up to the glow-in-the-dark phosphors. Small oddments of plastic. But four things are recognizable.

Chunks of concrete, maybe off an old Cannery Row sardine factory.

A gray sweat sock, red stripes at the cuff.

A flattened box of Brillo Steel Wool Soap Pads with Lemon Fresh Scent!

Several wadded plastic bags, which, Jay realizes, do resemble squid.

2015

Plastic bags everywhere. Saturday morning. Fort Ord Dunes State Beach. A Save Our Shores volunteer event. Black clouds, gales that steal the breath from your lungs, seas leaping like a million white hands. Jay's ten. A judge forced Dad to come: he threw a college kid off a pier for chucking bottles into the ocean. Dad picked up precisely one plastic bag before he got wind of some Greenpeace types prepping to dive under illegal boats to slash their nets. He took off to join them. Just the other day, Mom sighed that Dad's been doing this more often, while Nan and Eva mouthed the magic word: *emasculation.*

Dad didn't think to bring Jay, naturally, who's better off with the youth groups and old folks. Like Hewey. A humiliating desertion at first, but Jay's having fun tabulating his gatherings on the SOS scorecard.

Shopping bags / bolsas de comestibles = 44

"One whale, few years ago, France I think, three-hundred-some individual pieces of nonbiodegradable plastic they found inside it," Hewey says.

"Wouldn't that kill it?"

"Takes a while but yep. The whales start thinking they're full, so they stop eating. Pretty soon they starve to death. The only thing that'll stop whale extinction at this point is if we go extinct first. Think of that, son. People and their trash are doing what generations of whalers couldn't."

"Geez. That sucks."

Straws and stirrers / popotes y mezcladores = 22

"Two-hundred-some pounds of junk they found in one whale. In Scotland!"

"That's heavier than me."

"I'll say."

Bottles / botellas = 53

"Dad says I'm too small. Maybe I'd make good fish food."

The old man looks from under his safari hat. He's holding so much plastic he's practically made of it. Jay thinks of the plastic St. Christopher in Hewey's car.

"You *are* fish food, kid. All this plastic is getting in the way of our animal duty. Which is: we gotta eat each other, over and over, to keep this carousel turning round."

Finally lightning, an X-ray of the cloud's cardiovasculars. Everyone oohs. Raindrops like marbles. Beyond Hewey, the twisting seas, Dad on them, maybe under. Jay names it aloud. But what is he naming? The weather? A father?

"Storm."

Hewey, despite being solid plastic, winks at Jay.

"And you're the reason for it."

1591 PSI

Concrete, gym sock, Brillo pads, plastic bags. None of it fit to stop bleeding. Jay is, indeed, the storm: his mind bucks and rages until it grabs hold again of Architeuthis. Why did the squid attack him? He's neither predator nor prey. His Henderson wetsuit, though, probably *feels* like sperm whale. Which means the squid's target was never Jay's neck.

It was the neoprene.

Like his suit, Jay's hood is a 7mm Henderson, basically a tight black sock with a hole for his face and a bib that drapes over his shoulders. Without it, Jay's neck would have been gored to the trachea. Jay feels for the section of bib the squid mutilated, fearful his fingers will again graze the liplike folds of his wound.

There: a gash halfway down the bib.

Jay has a thought. Nothing seals to skin like neoprene.

If he could only cut a swath off the lower bib.

Because Mitt despised dive knives, Jay's got nothing to cut it with. Why couldn't the stupid whale have swallowed some fucking scissors? Jay's suddenly livid. He slams his right hand into the mire.

A cord of pain envelops his whole arm. He screams so loudly he nearly loses his regulator. He springs his hand back up. Squints at it in the dim glow.

Wait. Hold on.

There *is* something sharp in here.

1566 PSI

Jay grabs the squid beak and pulls.

A tongue of black blood droops down his palm.

Jay pulls harder, wresting the beak side to side.

Kaleidoscopes of pain light the dark.

Difficult not to hold your breath against such agony.

Palm meat squishes.

Breathe sleepy, breathe sleepy.

A pop, like an ice cube into water, as the beak clicks past bone.

A wedge of palm meat uncorks and fires into the sludge. Jay blurts, a sneeze of suffering, his right hand shivering, whole body convulsing in relief. It's out! The beak's out! Jay drops his face into the cold saltwater slurry, cooling his sticky face as he wolfs air through the regulator. He makes a series of fists with his right hand. Muscles torn and shrill—but it hurts less each fist.

Forget hurt. Keep going. Work to do.

Jay hinges his head into the few inches of free space between the stomach and its lagoon. He cups the bloody beak in his left hand and, with his injured right, pinches the rounded base and pestles it, a figure-eight grind, eroding the white muscle. Harder, faster. His punctured hand cramps.

With a moist crack, the mandibles separate. Jay drops the broader lower mandible and curls his fingers around the smaller, sharper upper mandible. Sucks that he's got to do this with his bleeding right hand, but he's right-handed. He grips and regrips the beak until he finds a hold he likes: the rear crest pinched between thumb and side of his middle finger, index finger curved atop the beak's hood. Pretty close to how you pitch a slider.

Jay notches the hooked tip of the beak into the hole the squid made in his hood bib. He's seen Mitt cut raw neoprene on worktables and boat decks, always with a utility knife—and even then it was a chore. Jay's got to do it in the dark with half a goddamn squid beak.

1545 PSI

He starts sawing. Easy does it.

An Architeuthis beak. "Diamond of the sea," Hewey called it. Harder than metal, unscratchable and unbreakable, Mitt once rhapsodized. Severs prey's spinal cords as easy as a knife through noodles. Squid beaks were the base ingredient of ambergris, the waxy lumps shat by sperm whales and used in luxury perfumes, every poor fisherman's dream, selling for roughly twenty-five grand per pound.

People used to carry ambergris to ward off the Black Death. Jay would carry it now if he could. He's ready to believe in any religion, any superstition.

He tries to control his hand. But the beak keeps flubbing from the bib as Jay's vision goes inky. Each time it's harder to slot the beak back into place. Twice Jay's sawing fist clubs the all-important wedged fin. The fin shudders, sloshing slime. One more clumsy clobber and it'll fall, and the next peristaltic wave will crush him.

Jay thinks of the squid's gigantic eyes. He tries to make his eyes that big.

And by accident gets the angle just right.

The neoprene purrs open as if by zipper.

A swath the size of Mitt's copy of *Cannery Row* is freed. Eyesight tunneling, alertness ebbing, Jay pulls the wetsuit collar away from the injury. No time to clean it, he's got to hope the saltwater did some disinfecting. He slaps the rectangle of neoprene over the wound. Might not stick there on its own. He hikes up his BCD, lets the cylinder weight press down, hopes blood will become the glue, then feels the hardening of exactly that.

Maybe it's wishful thinking: right away, Jay breathes sleepy again.

1512 PSI

(Well done)

Jay finds himself nodding. Then stops.

He just saved his life. His *own* life.

Mitt had nothing to do with it.

The squid beak, though? Jay has the desire to kiss it. The idea strikes him as comical. Even a dribble of humor gives him an adrenaline jolt. He brings the beak to lips numbed by methane. It clacks against his regulator, as close as he's going to get. Jay makes the best kissing noise he can around the plastic mouthpiece.

"Thanks, Beaky."

Beaky fulfills the naming standard of the other objects Jay's held dear. Blankie the blanket, Zankie the other blanket, Bear-Bear the bear. Through uncountable stitchings and stuffings, the power trio stayed plushy, good to cuddle with. But a harder object—the hardest, in fact—might be what Jay needs now. He's seventeen.

He holds Beaky, cold and wet, to his cheek. Tries to think.

The memory of Jay's bedtime talk with Mitt had been lost for years. Had it been knocked loose by skull trauma? Liberated from his mind via methane? Doesn't matter. What matters is he's got a hold on it now, the memory's tether repaired like his wetsuit zipper. There's more here he can use. He grips. Pulls. Unzips it.

2014

"Here's how you have to think of it, Jay. The teachers giving you a hard time? They're the predators. Now, in the ocean, predators have all the advantages. They're faster than you, they can track you, they can get at you from any angle. What options does that leave for prey like you? Do you know?"

Jay shakes his head. What tears remain roll in new directions.

"Option One is for the prey to accept their fate. You're a codfish. You were born to be a goner. But that's not the Gardiner way. Option Two, you form a group with fellow prey. Dolphin-style. The predator gets confused. It can't get all of you. For me and you, though, that means joining up with other people. Yuck. I mean, Hewey, *maybe*. Option Three, live in a body that's no fun to eat. You're a turtle. Stonefish. Puffer. Option Four, camouflage. To hell with that. We is who we is, right? That brings us to Option Five. My favorite option. You ready?"

Jay nods. Is he ever.

Dad leans in. Bedsprings zing like an electrical storm. The mattress tilts like the deck of a banking ship. It's not a hug. Jay isn't sure he even wants that kind of contact anymore. But it's in the vicinity. The affable shine of Dad's eyes hardens into flat white coins. Jay could reach out and take them, slip them beneath his pillow, the tooth-fairy ploy in reverse: take the money, leave the slumber. The paths of his tears have dried.

"Option Five. The prey becomes so dangerous the predators let him go."

1489 PSI

Jay can't cut his way out of the whale. PBS specials made that evident. With flensing knives the length of hockey sticks and the sporadic chain saw to buzz through ribs, it takes all day for biologists to hack through blubber, fat, and muscle. All Jay's got is his hands, Beaky, maybe forty minutes of air. And the knowledge, at last, of what must be done.

What did Jay do after Architeuthis was slurped into the second chamber?

He threw up.

What handy fun fact does Jay recall about whales and whalers?

Sperm whales often regurgitated squid when they were harpooned.

If Jay can give the whale a stomachache, it might vomit Jay right back into the Pacific.

(Stop)

"No. This will work. It's my only hope."

When the Mitt-voice said Jay had brought everything he needed with him, it was a lie. The squid beak had been waiting to meet him in the stomach's second chamber. Beaky had no problem cutting neoprene. Neither should it have a problem stabbing the stomach.

((Stop))

"Don't mind him, Beaky."

Don't mind Jay Gardiner, either, talking to his dead dad and half a squid beak like it's normal.

The stomach bites down. Jay flexes every muscle he can. But the fin brace holds, and Jay isn't flattened, merely slammed with an open-field tackle. He works through it. He's learning. The slider grip won't work for stabbing, it's too delicate. He runs his hands over Beaky, every curve.

(Jay)

(We want)

(To talk)

(To you)

Jay's feels energy transfer from the beak to his body. The sonic hallucination of his father has served its purpose. Jay's going to get *himself* out of this.

"You want to talk to me, huh? Instead of order me around? That's a first."

(Whales must eat)

"You eat me, I eat you. That's what Hewey said."

(We miss Hewey)

"You don't miss him. You miss his boats."

(We miss so much)

(We miss the air)

(We breathe it only in gasps)

"Then you shouldn't have killed yourself, huh?"

There's no safe grip. The bone spur on the back of the beak might pop through his palm when he stabs. But there's no other way.

(We have been looking for you Jay)

"Sending out clicks? Guess I didn't hear them. Because I'm not a fucking whale."

How to stab the beak with force? The confined space offers no room to rear back. He'll just have to slice and dig with what passion he can. His muscles pang and joints ache just thinking of it. This is going to be a real son of a bitch. Then again, Jay tells himself, with an adrenalized dribble of humor, he's a real son of a bitch, too.

(Why haven't you been in the water Jay)

"Why do you think? I go in once—*once*—and look what happens."

(The water is where we are born and where we die)

Jay prepares Beaky. Bites his regulator. Sweat rains off his lips.

"Where *you* die. Not me. Not today."

The whale goes sideways. Stomach trash splashes, seawater kicked as if from a boat's hull. Everything hits Jay: concrete, Brillo pad box, wet plastic bags slapping his faceplate. The whale rights, the sludge drops. Jay's still there, a whaler of yore, harpooned to a leviathan, dragged into the blue and back out again.

(Your plan is dangerous Jay)

With the loud, wet smack of the opening gullet, Jay is pelted with whale food. A baby squid splashes onto his shoulder, a school of fish tries to bury him in cold biology. Jay shakes his head like a dog to toss the fish aside. The baby squid he ignores. He won't be stopped.

(Haven't we helped you Jay)

"You've *never* helped—"

(What do we eat)

(What are we)

(Go back)

(Reach out)

"Those were only hints. Stuff I would've figured out anyway. I wouldn't even *be* here if not for you. I was out *looking* for you."

(Yes)

"Even though you *never* looked for me."

(We are looking now)

"You just assumed I'd always be there to order around."

(Did you not assume)

(That we would always be there too)

1435 PSI

The reply startles Jay. Didn't see that one coming. It's too hard under this duress to lie to himself, so Jay admits it, sure, it's true, he figured Mitt Gardiner would persist indefinitely, even post-diagnosis. He'd go on complicating Jay's life through high school, though after that, Jay would depart, stay away for years, take pleasure in knowing Mitt only learned of his successes secondhand, until finally they met again, some undodgeable occasion, probably Nan's or Eva's wedding, and they faced off at a church, Mitt and Jay, suits and ties, grown men, the years apart having strengthened the junior and weakened the elder. Jay with a whole life ahead; Mitt gazing backward at regrets. Mitt would swallow his pride and ask Jay to stay with the family, not at a hotel, and Jay, magnanimous hero, would accept, but with an eyebrow that said it all. No more telling me what to do. No more telling anyone. No more *Sleepers, arise!* We Gardiners awake when we want.

Jay's played out the fantasy a hundred times. He'll never get to live it: Mitt's suicide finished off any dreams of triumph. It wasn't enough that Jay had to live according to Mitt's design. Now he's got to die like Mitt wants, too.

"You always wanted to be the big man. Well, you got it. Sixty tons."

(There is no weight in water)

"Your blubber? My BCD? Same thing, huh?"

(Here we are of the same weight)

"If that's true, then you're a useless piece of shit like me. Can't trim a sail. Can barely carry your cylinder."

(There need be no struggle when we are all the same weight)

"Work till the hour of the pearl! Be stronger! Be bigger! Stop crying! Stop crying! Stop crying!"

(A whale has an eye on both sides of its head Jay)

"What? You're not even making—"

(It cannot see what is directly in front of it)

This is about Mitt, Jay thinks. About anyone obsessed and righteous. Geniuses. Scientists. Artists. Renegade divers, too. If people of this caliber looked straight ahead, right at their tedious loved ones, the whole world would suffer. That's the message.

And it's bullshit.

Jay is sick of being the one bent toward breaking.

The eaten can't cave to the eaters forever.

He brings the beak back to stab, waiting for his moment.

((((JAY DO NOT))))

((((JAY WE CANNOT CHANGE OUR NATURE))))

((((JAY THINK WHAT WE WILL DO))))

2021

Instead, he finds himself thinking of something else.

Eight months ago. Eight days from his seventeenth birthday.

"So pretty," Mom says. "Your father would have loved it."

Jay gestures at Highway 1, a half block from the cemetery. Trucks scream past.

"Yeah, he loved highways. Dead possums. Tire rubber."

"Stop it," Nan says. She's after therapist-mandated closure, knelt beside Dad's tombstone like an actor in a movie. "She means the ocean."

The ocean's there, technically, across Old Salinas River, over the dunes of Moss Landing Beach. But it's Christmas Day, four months after Dad's death, and cold as hell, wind nibbling Jay's nose. The ocean is lost inside gray haze. What's visible is Dad's headstone, not granite, not marble. Concrete. The dates like accusations: *1965–2021*.

Dad would have loved it? No, he would have hated this Christian charade. One day, it will befall them all. Jay imagines four other stones and their inscribed birth years. Mom: *1970*. Nan: *1998*. Eva: *2000*. Jay: *2005*.

On the other hand, a different inscription: *ZARA* tattooed on Dad's biceps. Hadn't that been proof of love? Mom once told Jay and his sisters how wild Dad was when they met, how he'd looked forward to settling himself down, to *settling* down, to having kids, to being a father. Mom's no liar. Yet Jay struggles to believe it.

He struggles with a lot these days. Shame for what he didn't do for this dying father, guilt for how he hasn't been there, not in the flesh, for his mother and sisters. Something is building inside him. He doesn't know what yet. But he's got to make it right. Some gesture, something brave or valiant, that will show everyone he's sorry in ways that words can't, especially coming from his inartful, inarticulate self.

Eva lays her cheek against Dad's stone. The pom on her stocking cap bobs in the wind.

"I hate that he's not down there," she pouts.

Nan scowls at Jay like Dad's missing body is his fault.

Jay sighs, gray over gray, and gazes over the garden of stones. Mom dragged the lot of them here, tetchy in a compact car, past hand-painted signs for fried artichokes and sweet cherries, so she could feel Christmas like a punch. Her favorite holiday, an excuse to spoil the kids and revel in their joy, no matter that Dad detested it. Sheeplike singsongs, travel pollution, wrapping-paper waste, profane capitalism. Only cemeteries, Dad said, were a bigger swindle.

But weren't there moments? Jay glimpses them hiding in the fog. Dad accepting the Santa hat one year, using a strand of garland to fashion a bright red beard. Another year, tired on the carpet, letting Jay run his new toy car across the daredevil planes of his big body.

Now the daredevil himself is gone.

Jay notices the dirt of new graves, ones planted with actual corpses, is lightly domed. Must be for the same reason beached whales sometimes rupture, the expansion of putrefying gas. He thinks of nets hoisted by fishing boats, bloated with fish, pustules ready to pop. He thinks of an old sea urchin sting, his foot inflamed twice its size, how badly he wanted to lance it.

He thinks of Mom, on his birthdays, describing his overdue birth, the C-section.

When things pull taut: that's when you make your cut.

1401 PSI

Jay stabs the beak as the clenching stomach meets him halfway with ten times the force. Beaky splashes through the mire, impaling the stomach floor with a wet rip, a squirting squelch. The stomach springs away, and for one incredible second Jay's weightless, touching nothing.

Then, crash. His steel tank pounds his tender spine. His regulator jars from his mouth. He takes a mouthful of cold saltwater and colder jelly, but also liquid warmth as thick as ketchup.

Whale blood.

Blood that he, tiny warrior, drew.

Jay braces for his plan to work. For him to be vomited out. Instead, the whale goes perfectly straight. Clumps of muscle and swells of fat mobilize into missile calibration, everything a cog or cable. Digestive slorps and fizzles go silent, all that's left is the refrain of *BAUM, THROOSH*—and the echo of Mitt's last warning.

((((*JAY THINK WHAT WE WILL DO*))))

Jay's shaken hard, rib cage ringing with G-force. He stuffs his regulator into his bloody mouth as he's bombarded with fish, squid, trash. A Niagara roar fills his ears, deafening despite the muffle of meat and fat.

The whale's doing what whales do when they get scared. Mitt tried to warn him.

The whale is hiding.

The whale is diving.

Idiot. Loser. All Jay's ever done is fall.

2014

Off the front porch, Nan's shove, six whiskery stitches.

2015

Off the dock at Breakwater Cove, Dad's face lobster-red as he hauls
him out.

2016

Off his bicycle, pedals busted, dreams of future escape dashed.

2017

Off the honors list, grades in the gutter.

2018

Off the minds of his friends, he's always aboard *Sleep*.

2019

Off the map, lost, no compass except Dad, Dad, Dad.

2020

Off his rocker, everyone says, for leaving home at age fifteen. But Jay knows it's the right move. He'll rebuild himself. Find himself. Be found by others. Reconnect with friends. Figure out a love life. Repair his grades. Set up a future he wants. Harden those lungs softened by too much crying, too much mothering. He'll show them all.

1348 PSI

Instead, Jay Gardiner will die as Mitt Gardiner died, flotsam in the ocean abyss.

He's slugged to the back of the stomach, nowhere to go, spine cracking against tank steel, limbs tangled, femurs pulling cartilage from their pelvis pockets. Fish wiggle in Jay's face, baby squid suckers fatten along his mask.

What Jay feels most is a red coal of grief inside his heart. It's what people must feel inside a plane about to crash, a toddler rage at all the things left undone or unfinished. In Jay's case, a mother left to believe her son's death was a suicide, too, that she'd failed *him*, when Jay was the one who'd failed. Sisters he'd unfairly cast as villains, first because of their enviable ease with Mitt, then because they had been right about Jay's self-absorption all along.

Half-recalled facts pierce the blur. Sperm whales spend

(Sixty-two percent)

of their lives diving to depths of

(Ten thousand feet)

while the human body begins to struggle at anything past

(One hundred and thirty feet)

The wetsuit, BCD, tank, console, it's costuming, a joke. Open Water I taught Jay the volume of air a diver breathes is halved every thirty-three feet. With the whale heading down at

(Three to four knots)

(Twice that if scared)

(And we are scared)

he's got, what? Minutes left to live? There's no way, or reason, to fight.

Jay closes his eyes. Focuses on breathing.

And can't get enough air. His lungs are contracting.

Like that, he barely feels his body. Blame his heart, beating at one-third the normal rate.

Jay tries to let himself go—to fate, to nature, to water.

He's got time to arrange his final thought.

What would he like it to be?

2021

San Carlos Beach, July Fourth, Mom and Jay's aunts. Jay hasn't seen Mom much over the year since he left home, and still feels shame over favoring the company of women, but he's happy nonetheless, age sixteen, drinking a margarita. Covid-19 numbers have dipped; the Delta and Omicron variants have yet to explode; revelers are reveling. Mom reaches over, pretty under glistening skyrockets, smelling like her purse—leather and ballpoint pen—and brushes salt from his chin, his scarless chin, and says, "You don't look anything like him." She wouldn't say this if Jay didn't, in some ways, *act* like him, so it's both bad and good, the whole world in a pinch of chin, and in the dark he cries tears of light, purple, pink, yellow. Funerals are celebrations. It's a memory he can die with.

1334 PSI

Pressure builds the deeper you dive, basic stuff, but this is beyond. Jay's joints are smooth butane flame. His body is sheathed in cement, curdling, crusting. It should be scary. He's dying. But that's the nice thing about nitrogen dissolving into your blood, it dissolves your good sense along with it. Jay feels like he did that July Fourth on San Carlos Beach, tipsy on margaritas, five weeks before Mitt killed himself. All his worries, poof.

Pressure, harder, his ears, sinuses, dental roots. That's okay.

The seams of his skull pull apart. Doesn't mind.

A dull bang inside his right ear. Crackling sonic fire through his skull and hood. His right eardrum has exploded. Jay smiles, tastes the bitter cherry of collapsing lungs.

Everything's fine.

1305 PSI

With the eardrum goes Jay's equilibrium. No up. No down. No near. No far. The whale moves not in any specific direction but all directions at once. That feels right. The sperm whale is everything to everyone. Always has been. Food, oil, devil, god.

Inscrutable monster.

Only a father.

Jay floats in their mingled ether.

(There need be no struggle when we are all the same weight)

This delicate repetition is Mitt's lullaby, offered at a new bedside. Now that Jay's finished fighting, he gets it.

They *both* felt it.

The impatience. Frustration. Irritation. Exasperation. Anger. Bitterness. Disgust. Derision.

The war between him and his father was never a war at all.

A series of skirmishes at most, which only felt significant because their eyes were on the fronts of their heads and never the sides, where the grandeur of life could have been better viewed, the thrill of every falling leaf and stinging wasp and crashing rain. Even their setbacks were magnificent and their bloodshed stirring, all of it working together in a machine called family.

Universes inside a single whale.

Universes outside it.

Jay Gardiner, a single star, flaming, falling.

But hadn't the sights been spectacular?

Didn't the hurts hurt bad?

Wasn't the love, the times he got it, the loveliest?

There is no fathoming the fathoms. All you can do is map the minuscule, memorize it, use it to predict infinity: the shimmering galaxies in the scales of an artedius fish, the solar storms of a moon jelly's gastrodermis, each bobbing kelp the stem of an ocean god's eyeball. This is how Mitt cycled his life, in rhythm, in patience, the same beaches, the same waters, the same subaqueous stretches. It's what he tried to teach Jay, clumsily, often disastrously. Jay never got it till right now, busy dying.

If you can't know what's right in front of you, you can't know what's beyond you.

1283 PSI

"I should have listened."

(We should have learned to speak)

"I should have known."

(We should have been a better teacher)

"I should have understood."

(We should have allowed confusion)

"I wish we could start over."

(We wish it too)

"I'm going home now, right?"

(Yes you are going home)

Even at the edge of death, Jay knows the figures. Seventy percent of the planet is water. Most of that water is deep ocean. The origin of everything. Less than 5 percent of the deep ocean is mapped. Humans know more about Mars. Anything could be down there. Therefore, everything is.

Heaven, Mom would insist. Hell, Hewey would chuckle.

The trident symbols at the crest of the whale's throat could be sunbursts. Or pitchforks.

Jay gets it. Heaven and hell are the same: the ones you love. Mom, her kindness and forgiveness, her secretly delivered candy and R-rated movies when he was little. Nan and Eva, bulldog protectors, ass-kickers to bullies, pushing him to do better, be better, adoring him even when, to the contrary, he got worse. All of them are the reason he's here, the reason he's dying.

He'd do it all over again.

His brain's not working so good now. Ditto his hands. Jay's gone too long without equalizing the pressure in his mask. He feels what's called mask squeeze, the air inside the plastic shriveling, turning into suction. Next, his eyeballs will pop out into his faceplate. Gross stuff like this is what young divers talk about.

"My eyes . . . I . . ."

(Shh)

(Your eyes saw so much)

After that, Jay's ribs will snap like a handful of twigs. If not already punctured by ribs, his lungs will collapse. After that, the crawlspaces of his sinuses will implode like lightbulbs, his face crumpling into debris.

"I . . . had . . ."

(You experienced a lot)

(More than most)

(Shh)

1254 PSI

Yes, shh. Jay nods. He won't be recognizable as human when he arrives where the whale's going. Will that expedite a Mitt-like reincarnation? Jay's unraveling mind finds sense in incoherence. How did he never see it before? The reason whales are so large is they absorb anything that dies in the shared plasma of the sea. Lots of vertebrates crawled from the ocean onto dry land. But whales turned *back*.

This doomed them—or blessed them?—to travel up, down, up, down, a convenient elevator between worlds for souls in transition.

Jay thinks of the life-sized whale sculptures in the Monterey Bay Aquarium. The photos he's seen of other sculptures in San Francisco, Santa Fe, Hawaii, Paris. The ninety-four-foot statue hanging in the American Museum of Natural History. The stuffed Malm Whale in Sweden, once outfitted with chairs so patrons could sit inside it and contemplate existence. Even the *Voyager 1* spacecraft, launched in the seventies in hopes of finding alien life, carries a golden record of whale song.

Memorials superior to anything Jay saw at the Carmelite Monastery.

Because deep down, humans know.

It is why Mitt's mug said *SAVE THE WHALES*.

It's only fair. When we die, the whales save *us*.

Jay smiles. Good memories are all around. It only took dying for him to rub the sleep from his eyes and see them clearly again.

His other eardrum rips apart, softly, distantly, bubbles through a straw.

2014

"You probably think I'm unhappy. Miserable."

Monastery Beach. Hour-long trek through the brilliant kelp, everything on proud display. A rare sunflower star. Delicate feather duster worms. Dark purple sea hares. A gigantic lingcod. A monkeyface eel the size of a boa constrictor. A duo of acrobatic harbor seals. Now Jay and Dad are on their backs on the hot, pilly sand, ignoring sandflies, wetsuits peeled to the waist, sparkling with salt, midday sun licking ocean from their navels. Steinbeck's words tattooed across Dad's belly feel true: *OUR FATHER WHO ART IN NATURE.*

"I don't know."

Jay's nine. How do you respond to statements like that?

"But there's satisfaction in sitting still. Most people, they're never satisfied. They get a nice car and, pretty soon, the nice car's not nice enough. It's leftover survival instinct, probably, something to keep the species developing. Your mom's like that. Your sisters. Doesn't mean they're bad, they're just— They don't know how to just *be*. There's these guys in *Cannery Row.* One day you'll read it. Bunch of hobos, but they know how the pursuit of money, it'll kill you. They have a little shack and they're happy. They take life as it is. Not how they wished it could be."

Jay's wary of this placid tone. But it gets him thinking.

What if what Dad said is true? What if a life full of poor choices could be washed from you every time you dipped under?

Dad shifts contentedly in the sun and sand.

"I bet if you did the math, Jay, I'm the happiest guy you know."

2010

Dip.

Jay and his sisters in the yard, cool grass at their necks, Dad, too, excited by the clarion sky, pointing out the Big Dipper, Little Dipper, Orion, Gemini, one for each of them, inscrutable space revealed as a mirrored home. Though no home could be better than this one.

2012

Dip.

A dump truck near the docks, and of course Dad knows the driver, he knows everyone, and Jay gets to sit on Dad's lap inside it, a Tyrannosaurus growl vibrating the wheel, Dad's hand over his own to direct the gear shift, what power, what love, both of them the same skeleton.

2014

Dip.

Hideous haircut. Mom's idea. Buzzed, when all Jay's friends wear it long. Dad passes through the kitchen, eyes the pouting Jay. Next time he passes, Dad winks and slaps onto Jay's head the scuffed old San Jose Sharks cap he's coveted since birth. No words. Words aren't needed.

2015

Dip.

Mom's bought a garage-sale guitar, five bucks, and she can play it? She's crooning songs she liked as a teen, Nan and Eva laughingly booing her cheesy choices, Jay grinning but wary of Dad nearby until, against all odds, he belts out Tom Petty's "Free Fallin'" at top volume.

2017

Dip.

Jay's starving, time to go home. From afar, he spots Dad not scrubbing himself of dock scum but under an upside-down rowboat propped like a tent, sharing sardines with a homeless man like they're old friends. Jay's hypnotized by the grins, the jokes, the laughter.

2018

Dip.

Jay and Dad sharing an umbrella at Del Monte and Alvarado, waiting for a guy who has Dad's paycheck. Jay's miserable, it's pouring buckets. Suddenly Dad closes the umbrella over them, opens it, closes it, Jay shrieking with the wetness, then hanging on to the umbrella as if for life, imagining the flapping will lift them off into the sky and over the sea.

1228 PSI

Dip.

Jay feels like he's exploding with remorse, all these lost memories. But it's probably the pressure. His eyes bulge on the edges of their lids. He closes them to delay eruption. His skull balloons. His bones croon like humpbacks. His cartilage goes *TAK TAK TAK*.

Pay attention. Feel every bit of it. Know what it is to lose your legs, to return to water, to become a chauffeur of souls.

Turn Jay Gardiner into a tale that never ends.

But this isn't what happens.

Jay feels the hard slam of a book.

Could be Mitt's *Cannery Row*.

Or Hewey's Torah, Qur'an, New Testicle.

Or a book being read right now, the reader gobbled up.

It's all those, and the whale, too. With a burly twist, it halts the dive that should have ended Jay's life. A whole ocean of frigid froth rushes past with a bowling-alley boom.

1205 PSI

The crumpled pile of Jay's body is thrown forward, a series of cruel gymnastics: knees to face, torn back muscle like burned rubber, head driven into the sludge of crunchy crustaceans. He'd skid like this for miles if the stomach didn't grip him like a wet sheet. His scalp drives into the gullet end of the stomach. His neck levers hard, his head's about to snap off—

The whale goes horizontal. The crushed wad of Jay's skeleton telescopes out, he's jumbled and shaken but alive, not paralyzed, not gouting blood. He digs a hand into the stomach tissue just to hold something. His other hand still holds Beaky. He holds it harder, good-luck charm, totem, friend. If he has Beaky, everything will be all right.

No: the whale flexes, a torque that stirs Jay like batter. The most violent movement the whale's made yet, that's no good, there's no reason it should be—

PWUD

Thunder at the level of *BAUM* and *THROOSH*, even through the carnage of Jay's eardrums. An impact tremor ripples through blubber, meat, and organs; Jay receives it like a two-handed shove as the whale sheers through water gracelessly. What kind of thing could toss this colossus, make it thrash in panic?

Maybe an avalanche of boulders off the canyon wall.

Russian submarines ramming.

World's end, the whole enchilada folding.

None of that. The answer squeaks through the pressurized lobes of Jay's brain.

Sperm whales only appear immortal. They die like anything dies. Mitt relished pinning the blame on humans. Earth's old fleet of harpooners. Modern Japanese whalers with harpoon cannons. The quiet harpoons of climate change. Some sperms get struck by ships. Some get tangled in nets and starve. Some, though, the unluckiest of behemoths, are killed by their only natural predator.

2014

"Orcinus orca!" Hewey cries, then translates the Latin. "Bringer of death!"

"Wolf packs of the sea," Dad grumbles. But he lodges his elbows on the rail and watches. Once in a lifetime do you get to see a feeding frenzy like this.

The killing takes two sickening hours. It takes all the mettle in Jay's nine-year-old body not to curl up on the deck. Fifteen orcas, by Dad's cataloging, tear apart a gray whale, their black-and-white bodies slithering beneath a kicking sea. The gray whale fights, slaps its flukes, tosses water some thirty feet. But hundreds of swarming gulls—the ocean's vultures—telegraph how it's going to end. Orcas fork off with maws full of red muscle. The oceans bobs with icebergs of white blubber.

1176 PSI

Jay has no way of knowing the number of orcas attacking. What he does know, per one of Mitt's old reports, is that an orca in the South Atlantic was tagged diving three thousand feet, close to sperm whale depths. Jay's whale—when did he start thinking of it that way?—is nowhere near that deep. Only deep enough to inflate Jay's body with enough pressure that one more orca impact will detonate his head like an overstuffed bag of trash—

PWUD, PWUD

Nope, Jay's still here, not exploded and too bad, he's radioactive with pain, teeth squealing in their sockets, bones shrieking like nails being yanked from wood. The whale takes more hits—*PWUD, PWUD, PWUD*; heart rate hectic—*BAUM BAUM BAUM*; pulse wilding—*THROOSH THROOSH THROOSH*—

Jay's the same, heart a kick drum, pulse whipped to cream, head fired like a billiard ball, regulator chiseling his gums. He tastes blood, surely his, but then, in the glowing mist, watches the whale's gullet open and let in a crimson gush. It hits Jay hard as chain mail, painting his face mask red. His mouth full of whale blood now, colder than his own, thicker, saltier.

The orcas are killing Jay's whale.

And there's nothing he can do about it.

1153 PSI

Since the spotting from Hewey's boat, Jay has feared orcas as he's never feared sharks. Sharks feel to Jay like busted robots: empty eyes, shattered-glass teeth. Orcas, though, inspire the worst heiliger Schauer Jay has ever felt. With their tidy, evenly spaced teeth, pillowy pink tongues, and cheerful faces, orcas look like malevolent clowns, so embroiled in the religion of death their markings resemble skulls.

Orcas typically target sperm whale calves first. After that, the sick. So why this whale of ungraspable size and might?

Jay knows why; it hurts to know.

Because the whale is old.

Jay's thought many things of Mitt Gardiner. *Weak* was never one of them. But is it not true? All those scars. Those old wounds. The aging body. The cancer. Mitt *was* weak, had been for a time now. Meanwhile at the Tarshish place, Jay only grew stronger, more solidly his own. But at what cost?

He thumbs his regulator, voiding blood, sludge, mucus. He wishes he could scream up the whale's throat, scare the attackers into believing they'd chosen the only demon-possessed whale in the ocean.

If diving has stopped, there's a chance that he might live.

That they *both* might live.

Jay realizes he's no longer fighting only for himself.

2016

"People want to fire me, it's no skin off my back. What's a job? A gimmick of industrialized society. A hamster wheel you gotta turn to get your kibble. There was a time, before either of us were born, when you shared with your community what you had, where everyone's skills were valued. That quality—you know what it's called?"

In the truck just hours after Dad got axed from the charter-boat job, the whole 9/11-was-good-for-whales debacle. One of the best jobs Dad's ever had but he's taking it well, munching sardines, being philosophical. Better yet, Jay, age eleven, *does* know what the quality is called, thanks to a word taught to him by the school librarian.

"Benevolence." Jay butchers it.

"Benevolence. Good. Or altruism? Or just plain kindness? We should all take a page from the whale, Jay. Whales protect. And not just other whales. You won't believe all the different species whales protect. Take a guess."

"Dolphins?"

"That's right. And seals. And sea lions. And guess who else? Guess who else has gotten into danger, again and again, and hasn't deserved to have their ass saved? But who, nevertheless, gets saved by whales again and again? One guess."

Jay knows. His middle school once hosted a biologist guest speaker who talked students through the video she shot of a fifty-thousand-pound humpback tucking her under its flipper and chaperoning her back to her boat, from which she discovered a tiger shark on the prowl. Kids gasped. Jay, too. There are more tales of whale heroism around Monterey Bay, the biologist said proudly, than anywhere else in the world.

Has to be due to the canyon, Jay thinks. Our forgotten origin. The one place where every species in the world is family.

1126 PSI

Live, he's got to live. He can only do that if the whale lives, too. *Save the whales*: not just an outdated slogan anymore.

PWUD, PWUD

"Tell me what's happening."

(Death)

"No. Listen. How many are there?"

(Many)

PWUD, PWUD, PWUD

"Hit them back. Use your flippers."

(No good)

Jay knows the whale is right. Smaller whales like humpbacks have fifteen-foot flippers, solid muscle, capable of killing an orca with a single blow. But the major whales—the sperms, the blues—are evolved to focus their biology on diving, nothing but diving, at the expense of fleeing or fighting a predator swarm.

PWUD, PWUD

"Run away."

(Tail ripped we cannot)

PWUD, PWUD, PWUD, PWUD

"Call the others."

(There are no others)

"The ocean is full of them!"

(We are male)

Jay gets it. Sperms are as social as dolphins, but the adults in their pods are almost wholly female, twenty or thirty caring for their young, rotating babysitting duties while others dive deeper than the calves can manage. Around age four, the male children drift away, form bachelor groups, until the largest males fade into the isolation of polar waters, wandering alone.

Jay's whale has been away from its family for a long time.

But family doesn't forget. For worse, but also for better.

The stomach rumbles and wrestles with orca concussions. Jay places his numb lips to the shaking tissue, whispering straight into the flesh.

"Call to them. Try. They might be ready to hear."

1099 PSI

PWUD PWUD
   BAUM
   PWUD
   THROOSH
   PWUD PWUD
   BAUM
   PWUD PWUD PWUD
   THROOSH
The whale's not even trying.

It's August 10, 2021, all over again, Mitt Gardiner tipping from another rowboat.

1072 PSI

Click codas fire from the whale's bulwark of oil, the speaker system for the Earth's loudest sounds. Even insulated in stomach meat, Jay is deafened. His bones quake inside their muscle scabbards. This is no blunt-force *TAK*. These are phrases, descriptions, solicitations, directions, all of such force they shake fissures into the canyon.

CLANG-CLANG, PREEEE

"Keep going!"

SQUEEP, PIP-PIP-PIP

"Yes!"

REEK, HRONK

CRACK-CRACK-CRACK-CRACK-CRACK

Any single sperm whale shares a six-mile signal range with an estimated seven thousand others. That's the science. Jay's staggered anyway. The speed of the response, the lack of fear. The erratic orca drubbing cuts off as Jay's whale is thrust through the water, harder than ever before but with confident purpose.

It's the nudges of fellow giants. Not just a cluster but a full armada of sperm whales, undoubtedly females, nosing their way into battle, shielding their injured elder with younger skin and stronger muscles and the diffused targets of their extra tons.

The whale rolls as the other sperms, taking orca attacks, rebound into it.

Jay is sprawled. He pushes back onto his elbows.

"What's happening? What's happening?"

(Star)

Is this bloody delirium?

"No! Don't die! Hang on!"

(We are a star)

The whale rolls, Jay rolls, his brain rolls, and the meaning of it rolls right in.

Marguerite.

1047 PSI

Mitt talked about it. Hewey talked about it. Outnumbered by ambushing orcas—eight versus twenty, four versus twelve, nine versus thirty-five—sperms enact the "marguerite formation" defense: heads together, tails out, a star-shaped rosette that protects their vitals as they slap orcas with their mighty tails. If one of the whales is dragged away by an orca, a couple of its brethren break off, flank the injured whale, and lead it back, tucking it into the center of the star.

Right now, Jay's whale is that center.

"Stay in the middle!"

(Beautiful star)

"Are you hurt?"

(Remember the stars)

"Let the other ones do the fighting!"

(On the deck do you remember)

On the deck of *Sleep*? The night Mitt tried to get Jay to cut his own skin and paint his face with blood? Why would Mitt want to bring that up? It's not some buried morsel of info like the marguerite formation or a blocked-out life event like the methane poisoning at Sheol Landfill. It's something Jay has agonized over for two years.

That's how he knows the sky did, in fact, scintillate with stars that night, basting Mitt's bronze skin a cadaverous white, the blood sigils on his cheeks gone purple-black. The stars acted as lanterns, lighting Jay's thousand-foot swim back to Fisherman's Wharf #1, ensuring he lived so that, one day, he could swim back.

And end up here.

1020 PSI

Jay does not see, but certainly feels, the rest of the siege play out according to the marguerite design. The orcas come in echelons, four or five charging from several hundred feet off. Lakes' worth of water are shoved by whale flukes as they swat back orcas. Individual attackers retreat for ten minutes before attacking again. Soon that ten minutes dwindles to two. Sperm skin is tough; it takes skill, luck, and tenacity for a few orcas to get their teeth into it, whip their heads, and come away with chunks. The injured are added to the star's center alongside Jay's whale. This leaves the points of the star more vulnerable. Many whales, if not most, are injured. It is possible some of them die. The orcas tire and take off with what meat they can.

The marguerite loosens.

Jay's curled beneath sloshing sludge, exhausted. Only distantly does he feel the nudges of the protector pod. Weaker now but somehow affectionate, proud of saving the old male from dismemberment. Not that Jay's whale has an optimistic prognosis. Though the stomach is dark, Jay can make out the red hue, feel its glue, smell its smell.

Half the liquid in the stomach is blood.

The whale clicks in gratitude, but it's frail.

tak

The whales begin to ascend. Pressure leaks from Jay's skull. Bones pop in relief, settle back into interlocking pieces. His eyeballs shrink back into their sockets. His lungs feel like crumpled paper released from a fist, but it's better than being in the fist. He takes bigger, easier breaths.

Outside, the fifty-ton angels nudge, swaying Jay's whale like a clock's pendulum, while their clicks become the second hand. The whale's time is passing fast now. But the females stick close, do what they can.

They are the whale's family now.

Which means the whale is home.

Jay wonders how it feels for Mitt, sender of so many clicks over his seven-month demise, to be the subject of such a reception, to feel the bodies of loved ones so close inside the ocean vast. There's nothing to hug in a stomach, but Jay does his best. He wants the whale to know he's here. At last, he's here.

995 PSI

A familiar splatter. Even injured, maybe mortally, the whale's instinct is to eat. From the direction of the esophagus, a soak of cold ocean water and a spill of silvery fish over Jay's bowed head. He turns his face to the side, one eye submerged, incapable of surprise.

He's surprised anyway.

A jellyfish. Scared, fast, racing across the kiddie pool. Jay's seen hundreds over the years. Ghost jellies, cross jellies, comb jellies. But this is Periphylla—a helmet jellyfish. Makes its home in the canyon's Midnight Zone, one-to-eight-thousand feet down. Periphylla rise into the Twilight Zone to feed. This one, however, got the bad end of the deal.

It's gorgeous. Bright pink. Its bell perhaps of dinner-plate diameter when inflated with water, which it won't be ever again. It's skittering, trying to go deeper, its conical grace malformed into a flabby disc. Twelve-foot-long pink tentacles stiffer than any jelly Jay met in his silly, shallow exploits. Jay watches it settle, coming to terms with an altered universe.

The Periphylla emits a red cascade. Not the warning reds of brake lights, stoplights, danger lights. The red of a rose bouquet, a gift of the earth. A gift to him. Jay smiles at it.

"We shouldn't be here."

The jellyfish isn't the whale. It doesn't respond. It does, however, appear to agree. It powers down its lifelight alarms. Gives its power to the whale, Jay hopes, which is still being escorted upward. Toward the surface. Toward hope.

968 PSI

Some concern about the bends. Open Water I's rules of thumb: don't ascend over thirty feet per minute spent under, pause for three minutes at fifteen feet below the surface. To these usual concerns add the nebulous factors of fatigue and dehydration. Point is, if Jay doesn't ascend gradually, he'll start to feel the sharp pain of bubbles in his joints, spinal cord, or lungs, even in his bloodstream and brain.

It's out of Jay's hands, to say the least. All he can do is breathe sleepy to stave off a bevy of lung trauma including, but not limited to, arterial gas embolism, mediastinal emphysema, and collapsed lungs. The fun goes on and on.

Also possible: there's nothing to worry about. Now there's a thought Jay never expected to have. From the feel of it, the whale heads heavenward like a hiker on a low-grade switchback trail, back and forth. Maybe due to the pod's docile escort. Maybe due to the whale's dire injuries. Or maybe due to the part of Mitt inside the whale, carrying the knowledge of exactly what Jay needs to stay alive.

Jay wipes his mask and reviews the stomach. Fish, slime, the jellyfish. Beaky secure in Jay's right hand. Dark blood occluding nearly all bioluminescence. Fin no longer bracing the stomach, but that's probably okay. It isn't likely the whale will feel like chewing food anytime soon.

Jay rotates, curls up, couching himself in the stomach's side. Feels all right. Like the sofas of friends he slept on after leaving home. A bed that can, if he's careful, fit two.

His hip scrapes past one of the concrete chunks. It's Jay's first quiet moment; he gives it attention. The concrete has troubled him since he first saw it. Everything else the whale swallowed floats. It makes no sense for it to go out of its way to scoop up concrete.

Unless the whale knew what it was doing all along.

2021

"Dive weights."

Hewey's reply to Jay's question about how Dad weighed himself down. Lots of things skitter through Jay's mind over the next ninety minutes as a startling number of people file through the funeral home, the twisty line of sailors, fishermen, and divers all there, hats in hand and pandemic masks on, to pay respects to a man whose body isn't even on the premises. Many give Jay blameful looks. Avoiding their eyes, Jay dwells on his dad's death. On *Cannery Row*, a good-natured story that, rather inexplicably, features four suicides in under two hundred pages. On how whales have been known to fill their stomachs with rocks—probably chunks of concrete, too—to weigh themselves down so they drown. Because their lives, without predator pursuits or the limitless expanse of an ocean, are no longer worth living.

2022

Yesterday. Elkhorn Dive Center in Santa Cruz. Jay suppressing butterflies, praying the clerk will give his battered Faber 120 the sticker he needs before she'll fill his tank. But she recognizes his last name, matches it to his face. Jay thought he'd be safe an hour north of Monterey. You bring up Mitt Gardiner in Monterey dive shops, all you get is jawing about what a great guy he was. It's like being nipped apart by sharks.

"Oh shit. Your dad's Mitt Gardiner. I mean, was Mitt Gardiner. Sorry."

Jay offers a gesture between a shrug and a nod. He can't be off-putting, he needs this lady's VIP sticker. She thins her lips, weighs the dynamic, leans her elbows on the counter.

"My first time solo diving, *really* solo diving, I was out on Point Lobos. And your dad was out there. And he saw me. Way across the cove, I don't know if he had Superman vision or what. And he gave me the fist—you know, the danger sign. He swam over and I recognized him and I was excited, but he looked like he was going to kill me. He grabbed my belt real hard and told me I was way overloaded with weights, he could tell by how I was moving. Like I said, my first solo. I think I could have been in real trouble."

"He probably thought you were cute."

It's a mean thing to say, an attempt to sever conversation. But the clerk doesn't get mad. She smiles, eyes pooling.

"He probably saved my life."

"That's good. That's great."

"I've told that story a hundred times and every time someone responds with a story just like it. Your dad probably saved a *lot* of lives."

Saved? Not ruined? It's the lesson of the funeral visitation all over. People did care. They saw the good in Mitt Gardiner. The same way Mom saw it, and Nan and Eva saw it. There's a chance, just maybe, that Jay has been the blinkered one.

945 PSI

Whale by whale, the pod departs. Jay feels farewell taps and the looser ride of an unimpeded ocean. The great male is deserted so it can finish the only job left after seventysome years of dominion.

The job of dying.

Jay checks his pressure gauge: 945 psi. Less than a third of what he started with. By scuba standards, he's supposed to ascend with 500 psi in the tank. He's heard of divers pushing it to 200. If the whale reaches the surface, Jay might technically pull off the ascent, not that it will help him escape the stomach. Just as likely, the whale will die before it breaches, in a shoal of blood every shark in the bay will taste. Jay will be ripped apart with the carcass.

Injured flippers, injured flukes, pounds of flesh stolen. The whale lists leftward. If Jay recalls first-aid class, arterial and pulse pressure will soon fall, and the heart will dramatically slow. Jay will feel its spasms through the stomach wall. Adjacent organs will panic, transform into individual wounded animals desperate for life.

The verdict by the dim neon light is that Jay's in no better shape. Hands burned, scraped by whale teeth, the right palm gored by Beaky. Gums torn up, teeth maybe bent or busted. Shredded eardrums like two toothaches. Bones fractured by the stomach's garbage-truck gnashing. Every alveolus of his lungs tortured. A 7mm strip of neoprene all that's keeping his neck wound from being mortal.

Jay rests his head into a pocket of tissue. A perfect fit.

He and Mitt never cared to witness each other's lives.

But they're doing a fair job of witnessing each other's deaths.

Witnessing is of limited value when there's no one to read the chronicle. Unless the story becomes its own teller, scribed through DNA, surfacing in Nan's and Eva's children, some knowledge in their guts of things sowed and reaped, lost and gained.

The participants could, at least, tell the tale to each other: Jay to Mitt, Mitt to Jay. It's the conversation they had in the alternate world where Jay stayed aboard *Sleep* instead of swimming for shore.

Don't sons have responsibilities, too?

The answer is yes, they do.

To hold their fathers accountable.

916 PSI

"Why'd you do it?"

(Eating is what we do)

"Not that. Why'd you have me? You already had Nan and Eva."

(We wanted a son)

"You didn't act like it. You acted like you wanted a servant."

(We must pass on the things we know)

"It didn't work. You see how it didn't work?"

(It did work)

"How?"

(You are still alive)

"Because I listened to what you said?"

(Yes)

"But if I hadn't gotten swallowed. That one-in-a-billion chance. All the stuff you told me would have been useless bullshit. Was it really worth it? For me to hate you?"

(Yes)

"Why?"

(Because you are still alive)

"You're still impossible to talk to. You know that?"

(You are also not easy to talk to)

"Whose fault is that?"

(It is easy to assign fault when you are angry)

"Why would I be angry? Do you think?"

(Because of us)

"That's right."

(Because we were not the father you wanted)

"That's right."

(What if the opposite is true)

"That I wasn't the son you wanted?"

(Yes)

"You don't get to choose. You get what you get."

(Yes)

"You had to deal with the son you had."

(And)

"And what?"

(And)

"And . . . I had to deal with the father I had. Is that what you want me to say?"

(Yes)

"It's not the same. One of us was an adult. It was your job to be better than me."

(We failed)

"I don't like this *we* you keep using. You don't get to share blame with a whale. The whale didn't do anything wrong."

(That is not the *we* we mean)

"You mean *we* as in *you and me*? Nuh-uh. I was too young to fail."

(For how long are you too young)

"We're dying. Both of us. And you're still blaming *me*. The kid."

(You were old enough to run away)

"Yeah. I was. And everyone thought I'd fail. And I didn't."

(So we agree)

"We agree what?"

(That you were not too young)

"I— I don't— These fights don't get us anywhere."

(We do not want to fight)

"Fight is all you ever did. With anyone. Everyone."

(It was not the world we wanted)

"Yeah. I guess we agree on that."

(We are sorry)

"About what?"

(The world might have been what you wanted)

"If I'd lived longer?"

(Yes)

"Maybe. Maybe this was fate. Maybe dying will be easier if I believe that."

(Two currents crashing)

"That's good. Sounds . . . cinematic."

(The crash is what creates a storm)

"If Hewey was right, and I'm the reason for the storm . . ."

(Good old Hewey)

"Does that mean *you're* the storm?"

(Beware trying to understand anything Hewey says)

"I just mean . . . you know . . . are *you* what happened to me?"

(Are you what happened to us)

"Okay. That's fair. We—"

(Suffer our own storms)

"But do the storms have to kill us?"

(Eventually they must)

"Were we always going to kill each other?"

(Is that what we have done)

"I don't know. But I *was* out hunting. For you."

(And we were out hunting for you)

"Okay, but how did it happen? Did the whale eat you first? Your body, I mean?"

(Whales eat many things)

"Dad, you're *dead.*"

(The water is where we are born and where we die)

"You said that before. But I don't get it. Are all things in the water connected? Something like that? Could I have just gone fishing and had this conversation with, like, a halibut? That would've been easier."

(Cetacean)

(Cachalot)

(Potvisch)

(Makko-kujira)

(Kit)

(Fálaina)

(Cetus)

(Leviathan)

(The whale is forever)

"I don't know. Sounds like something a whale would say."

(We do not understand)

"It's a joke. You always had a thing for whales. You preferred them to me."

(The whale is forever)

"You said it yourself. The only reason people wanted to save the whales was to make themselves feel better. Saving some little lizard wouldn't do that. But a whale's so big, so mysterious. That must mean it's spiritual, right?"

(You are close)

"I'm being sarcastic."

(But you are close)

"Fuck saving the whales. You could have saved *me*. I didn't even rate a coffee mug."

(Where are you)

"Unbelievable."

((Where are you))

"You've been asking that since I got here. I don't know what you want."

(((Where are you)))

"I'm in your stomach, asshole."

((((WHERE ARE YOU))))

"Don't yell at me! What is your problem that you can't see me? Maybe you saw your reflection in the ocean so long, it's the only face you recognize. No wonder you killed yourself. You got sick and finally had a reason to need me, but when you looked around, oops. Not there. Of course you'd want to fall off the boat. Join yourself at the bottom of the sea. It was weak. *You* were weak."

((((( )))))

"Ahh!"

((((( )))))

"My ears, you're—"

((((( )))))

"Stop it, stop it!"

((((( )))))

2021

"It's called a thoracoscopy. They cut a small hole in his chest and put in this camera tube. I guess it looked bad. So now they're doing a, let's see. A thoracentesis. A mouthful, huh? Because he's panting, he can't hardly breathe. They take this needle and drain the lung fluid. It's awful, Jay. And I know this is so hard for you. But it's all he says now: *Don't break my heart.*"

Voice mail from Mom. Jay listens once. Feels unwell. Swipe. Trash.

2021

Docs removing his pleural lining tomorrow AM
Then they scrape the tumor gunk from his lungs
Mom wants him to get an asbestos lawyer but he won't
Eva and I both back in town for this
Where are you Jay???

Texts from Nan. Jay surveys reaction emojis. Chooses the heart.

2021

"He's not going to make it. The survival rate's, like, ten percent. It's pretty fucking terrible, Jay. He's got this gross catheter thing to drain the yellow slime out of his chest. That's super fun. He can't do it himself 'cuz he's all fucked up by the chemo. Oh, and there's constant diarrhea, Jay. Constant vomit. And Mom gets to take care of all of it. Alone."

FaceTime from Eva. Jay says sorry, he promised he'd meet up with Chloe.

2021

"Extrapleural pneumonectomy. I'm getting good at saying it, huh? They're going to take out the whole lung, and the lining thing, and pretty much all the lymph nodes, and some of the diaphragm, and also the pericardium, which is the lining around the heart. It's really our best shot. He won't have much stamina. Definitely won't be diving again. You can imagine how he feels about that."

Phone call from Mom. Jay zones out. Rotten organs inside him, too.

2021

Did you even know he has NO HAIR? He's doing RADIATION now. There is NO POINT. He's torturing himself. And WHY. Why do you think he's doing this JAY. When he says DON'T BREAK MY HEART who could he be talking about JAY. Who is he staying alive for to see one more time JAY.

Email from Nan. A horror flick with jump-scares. Jay archives it as fast as he can.

891 PSI

The whale rises slightly with each switchback sway. Jay has never known a softer motion. It's astonishing such gentleness could come from a beast so grievously injured. The whale, of course, but Mitt Gardiner, too.

"I'm sorry."

(There is no time left to be sorry)

(There is no fighting when there is no way to win)

(We are dying now)

(There is no changing that)

(But you Jay)

(There is strength in you yet)

Part of Jay doesn't want to hear it. It's so warm here, so cozy. The two of them comfortable together at last. He pats around for his instrument console: 891 psi. Twentysome minutes of air. Those last few won't be pleasant. But he doesn't think there's a better place in the universe to be asphyxiated.

The other part of Jay—he can't help it.

He's received so few encouraging words from his dad.

(There is strength in you yet)

Yet—which means there was always strength in Jay and Mitt always knew it.

Time to use that strength. Whatever's left.

Time for Jay to fight like Mitt fought.

There's so much to live for. Maybe Mitt couldn't see it, but now, finally, Jay can.

He slides his left elbow under him. Experiments with his biceps. His arms convulse. But he holds a pushup pose. Fish, plastic trash, even the helmet jellyfish eddy past his mask. The tank's valve once again stretches the stomach. His whole body shaking now. Jay sucks canned air, a lot of it, then again, and again, new beads of sweat oiling his wetsuit. He bites the regulator.

"Now what—do I—"

(The last thing you saw before entry)

"What? I saw—you—the whale—"

(The last thing you saw)

"The . . . mouth? What?"

(The last thing you saw)

"The teeth—the tongue—I don't know what you—"

(The last thing you saw)

Like lightning: alabaster lines on charcoal flesh. That's right, it was the last thing Jay glimpsed before the Architeuthis tentacle dragged him into the gullet's blackout.

Two symbols etched into the top of the throat.

Each set like a five-pointed spear.

Jay's only considered the symbols in occult terms: demonic hieroglyphics, evidence of dreaming delirium. But it's simpler than that.

"Scratches."

(Yes)

"Something was in here before me."

(Yes)

"Something with claws. A seal."

(Yes)

"And it got free."

(Yes)

"Does that mean I can just . . ."

Jay looks straight ahead. Inches from his nose, the closed fist of flesh leading to the gullet, the entry point of everything swallowed, including him.

". . . climb out?"

863 PSI

Even after the throat widened, Jay's ride down it had been tight. Only the tug of the squid's leash had forced it. Wasn't going to be any easier the other direction. Jay thinks of taking off his BCD. Tough enough to do on a beach, though he might manage it. But how to bring along his tank *and* climb? It won't work.

Still, there are things he can remove.

The weight pockets along his waist are easy. He slumps to a shoulder and digs in. The D batteries are gone from when he dropped weights inside the whale's mouth, but there's some AAs in there. Twenty-seven grams each, if he recalls his googling.

He pitches them into the stomach.

Next, he reaches back and below, corrals the auxiliary regulator hose. His primary has lasted this long, and this extra dangler will catch on everything. Same with the BCD's power inflator: the plastic trigger, the dump valve, neither any use to his ruptured Oceanic. Jay wishes he could put Beaky back to work and cut away these unhelpful protrusions, but that would bleed his canister dry instantly.

Instead, he unbuckles a shoulder strap and threads the hoses through it. With the added bulk, it doesn't rebuckle easy. Jay pushes hard, all his weight. The hole in his palm squishes, rotating rings of fire, before the buckle clicks back into place. He gasps, heaves, does his anti-hyperventilation routine. There. Good. Two more obstructions gone.

Jay drags the last hose up to his face, the console.

The dials still glow. The depth gauge reads 70. Good, getting closer to the surface. The pressure gauge, though: 863 psi. Into the orange. Danger, danger. If he tucks this tube away like the others, he'll not be able to check how much air he's got left. Maybe it's better not to know. Maybe he should just fight as hard as hell for as long as he can, end of story.

Jay lets the console hang free.

One handhold to the outer world. Surely that's allowed.

Finally, the bone bag. Still suicide-clipped to the BCD.

Jay focuses and saws it free with Beaky. He feels the empty mesh fall away, sink into slime. Who could have guessed it? Never needed the damn bag to begin with.

838 PSI

The stomach's residual light is enough for Jay to tell the gullet sphincter is nothing like the one separating the stomach chambers. The
clutch of pink flesh is airtight and brawny, bigger than any single part
of Jay's body. He won't be able to get through it on raw effort alone.
Yet the idea of coming at it with Beaky's blade is too much like Mitt
lurching at Jay with his knife aboard *Sleep*.

"Can't you eat again? Then it'll open."

(A whale eats when a whale eats)

"I don't want to hurt you anymore."

(It is what must happen)

"If I cut you, will you dive?"

(We are not scared now)

(We are injured)

(We want air)

(We are surfacing soon)

"What if I cut you and you're never able to eat again?"

(It does not matter)

(We are dying)

"I can't."

(Do it)

"I *can't.*"

((((YOU GOT SOFT LUNGS JAY))))

811 PSI

Jay cuts.

He's mad. A dirty trick. Even dead, Mitt knows how to push him. Beaky's dark brown blade saws through tight wads of pink muscle, purple once it's split and drooling a thin, greasy fluid. The mouthlike orifice puckers tighter.

"Harder, Beaky."

Jay's arm burns from back-and-forth repetition. The in-out cluck of regulator air is loud and frantic. It's awful, an atrocity, slicing up this miracle monster, this floating angel worth ten million Jays. But he saws faster. Soft lungs. He will not have soft lungs.

"Harder, Beaky!"

Six-inch slice, a red radius through the fleshy coil. Jay dislodges Beaky, hears blood patter his wetsuit. The sphincter trembles and tightens. Jay aims, biceps wailing, and again jabs Beaky into the sphincter's nucleus. He begins sawing a second radius line, this one angled off from the first cut, so that when the second slice meets the sphincter circumference—

A thick pie piece of muscle, red as cherry, topples into Jay's mask, dangling by a hank of pale tissue.

Jay's lungs pound. His regulator rattles.

"Ha! Soft lungs? Those sound like soft lungs to you?"

No retort from Mitt, whose own lungs went soft from cancer.

Jay folds his knees up, tight, crouched at the gullet base.

But first.

With great care, he nestles Beaky into an empty BCD pocket.

Jay will take it from here.

786 PSI

Next problem. How's he going to make this climb if he can't see?

The stomach moat is clabbered with luminous fish. But Jay can hardly tote them up the gullet in his cupped hands. He needs something bigger and brighter.

Inches from Jay's right hand, Periphylla floats, dormant.

Vibrant pink gone nightshade. Arms like a patch of stomped grass. Dead?

Time to find out.

It's never a super idea to touch a jellyfish. Even when they're dead, they sting. Young wharf rats rank jellies like other kids rank kaiju. Japanese habu induce cardiac arrest. That's pretty dope. A sting from the tiny Irukandji causes unbearable pain, vomiting, and—get this—a feeling of inescapable doom. Australia's Chironex fleckeri always gets a shout-out, a single bead of its venom kills divers dead. At age twelve, Jay took a pink-yellow sea wasp tentacle to the hand, hurt like a bitch on fire and gave Mitt the excuse to proudly bust out his home-brew vinegar spray.

Jay thinks—*thinks*—Periphylla's sting is beelike, akin to a lion's mane jelly.

But he doesn't trust anything his brain coughs up right now.

He folds a knuckle and nudges the jelly's saggy bell.

It blasts red—then blazes bright white.

Jay draws back.

The jellyfish oozes sideways.

Jay inhales hard, real hard. He's got to touch this jelly again. Not only touch it. Choke-hold it. A tough idea to wrap his head around. Gripping a stinging jelly is like giving your hand to a hyena. Surefire pain. No way will he be able to hang on. He pictures his stupid diving gloves, playing hooky in the trunk of his car.

Bud of pressure in his brain. Shit. The fucking bends? Now?

No. Nothing like that.

It's a seed. An idea plants roots.

763 PSI

Jay sieves his hands through the garbage. By touch, he tallies the usual suspects: right fin, Brillo box, concrete, plastic bags.

Bingo: gym sock.

He weeds it from the slush. It's stiff with brine. Jay props himself on his elbows and uses both hands to knead and unroll it. The sock snickers as it flattens, as if crystallized in dried syrup. Jay takes the sock cuff in his right hand and inserts his left fist. When his knuckles reach the toe, Jay rolls his wrist, loosening the crust.

A sock puppet rises from the dead.

Jay nods. Good. Glances at the jellyfish. Heart hammering.

He touches his socked hand to the bell.

732 PSI

Twelve ropy jellyfish arms lasso his fist and forearm, pink stripes over sweat-sock cotton. Jay gasps through the regulator and swings his fist as far from his face as possible, barely eight inches, what a colossally stupid idea this was. The jelly beams white and ejects blue slime over Jay's mask.

Jay wipes it away, braces for another jet. A second passes. Okay. Two. Okay? Three. The jellyfish clings, but that's it. The sock is doing its job, acting like a falconer's glove, absorbing any venom Periphylla tries to pump into his hand. Chewing his mouthpiece, Jay scooches himself against the daggered sphincter. The jelly weighs nothing but Jay's unnerved by its rubbery grip.

The jellyfish's white light dims to red, then to its natural pink.

Hopefully saving it up for when Jay really needs it.

Jay pushes his head into the wedge carved into the sphincter. With its fresh injury, the organ is less a cinching circle than a floppy oval. The bleeding edges gum him like a mouth pulled of teeth. Still, Jay's mask and regulator hinder progress. He has to hold them in place while driving forward with his neck.

Jay's head pops into the esophagus.

A deep-space black.

The first thing Jay notices is the smell. It's different from the stomach's sewage funk. This odor's spiny, fishy.

Equilibrium's upsetting, too. The stomach buffered much of the whale's sway. Not the gullet. Every degree of the whale's bank or bend, every wobble of its damaged trajectory, Jay feels in the gullet, in the throttle of his brain inside his skull.

He threads his right arm through the sphincter gap, then the arm swaddled in sock and jellyfish. With his elbow like pliers, he widens the aperture enough to shove his shoulders past the clenching muscle. His body shudders to a halt. His tank's too big to fit through, just as he'd feared. No hesitation: Jay flattens himself, every inch the skinny kid Mitt never liked him being. He plants his bare feet into the stomach's crunchy goulash and pushes. The tank rams and tussles, steel on flesh.

Injured flesh, though: the Faber 120 is victorious. Jay's body surges.

He's back inside the esophagus.

Most of him, anyway. His lower legs remain in the stomach. Before he brings them up, he's got to deal with the tarry darkness. His absurd idea will either work or it won't.

Jay blindly moves a knuckle toward the jellyfish pasted to his left fist. Doesn't want to jab and scare it. Only wants to graze it, say hello. He learned from Mitt that Periphylla uses its bioluminescence to signal other helmet jellies. But Jay's seen for himself that it also flares up when alarmed. So that's what he's going to do. He's going to alarm it.

His knuckle skims across the muculent surface.

Periphylla blazes scarlet.

Let there be light.

709 PSI

Jay's left fist is a torch. Preposterous. Incredible.

"It worked! It fucking worked!"

Jay's dizzy with success. So giddy he feels deranged. This is how Hillary and Norgay must have felt summiting Everest. Jay focuses on breathing. Get a hold of yourself, Gardiner. Death is everywhere.

He pushes his jellyfish lantern into the space above.

He's held in his heart the ecstatic fantasy that he'd see all the way up the whale's throat, through its mouth, and into a pool of blue water shimmering with yellow sunlight. But whales don't swim around with their throats open. At rest, the throat is a deflated tube, same as any mammal. All Jay sees is flesh.

Jay tries to think. Throat's maybe seven feet long. Less than two feet wide when open. The upward angle feels forty-five degrees at best. Periphylla's red gleam muddles the colors, but the tissue around him looks pinkish, orangey, dotted with black, coaster-sized ulcers. Jay presses his free hand into the gullet wall. Slick and fibrous, like soggy, salt-softened driftwood.

He slides his hand upward. Porky bulges. Furrowed veins.

Handholds. Footholds.

Jay sees a lump the size of a wallet. Grabs it. Pulls his left leg into the gullet and probes around with his burned toes until they find a nodule to grip. Quickly he hikes up six inches. His head peels the throat open ahead of it.

Carefully, Jay slides his right leg inside. Quickly he jams his right heel into the gullet lining, toes searching. There: a fatty wrinkle. That's three grips he has now, the best he's going to do with the jelly occupying his left hand.

Jay sucks air and squints. Already the gullet's seven-foot length has been reduced to five.

He can do this. He can do this.

682 PSI

Midway through the climb, Jay acknowledges it's the most difficult physical act he's ever performed. Forget the swim away from *Sleep*, every dive he's ever done. His tendons go tight as string. Individual muscle fibers twang. Every wound coughs up blood. His tank is heavy as a silo, he's Sisyphus beneath it, breathing harder, devouring air, shredding what time he has left.

Failure here is far worse than some innocent splashdown. If the whale senses what it thinks is food in its gullet, it'll instinctively swallow, the throat popping wide, muscles squeezing Jay back into the stomach. He'll be too weak to make another attempt before his air runs out. He's got one shot.

He needs to be perfect. And careful. And fast.

How to do that when the waterslide you're climbing is alive? The throat shivers. Ripples. Teases handholds, steals toeholds. That's not the worst of it. Jay knows from Mitt's intercom info dumps aboard *Sleep* that whales inflate their lungs as they near the surface in anticipation of firing their blowholes. The throat passes right between the lungs; Jay knows this because he *feels* it, the ballooning of two piano-sized organs, squeezing him tighter.

Shoulders curled inward. Elbows touching. Fingernails clawing. Toes digging deep. Jay's a free-solo rock climber in a bottleneck. Easy does it. Breathe sleepy. He shoves upward through lax tissue. Like a kidney stone through a urethra. He's doing it. He's doing it.

Until everything goes wrong at once.

669 PSI

Periphylla's light winks out.

Jay turns cold in the gullet's heat.

"No."

Did it die? Did the jelly die on him? He shakes his left hand.

"Wake up. Wake up!"

Oh shit. Oh shit.

Jay can't see. Can't see handholds, footholds.

Too terrified to move. Sound smashes into him. *BAUM, BAUM, BAUM,* the giant fist of the heart pounding next door to Jay's body, each beat shaking Jay's fingers and toes from slippery tissue. Jay pushes outward with all four limbs, picturing himself as a human burr. He's got to snag. He's got to hold.

Then pain—a cramp.

Oh *shit*. Oh *shit*.

The muscles of his left foot feel lashed to a medieval torture rack, pulled thin, hard as steel cable. If Jay releases that toehold, he's finished. But he needs to stretch the foot, roll it, massage it, all those things Mitt taught him. Mitt—wait—where did Mitt's voice go? Did his dad and the whale die, too, just now, the carcass ascending only via momentum? No, please, no, he can't be alone in here, not with the thud and wallop, the tendon-chiseling pain.

Jay slams his head against the throat, again, again, distraction from agony.

Screams through his regulator.

And chokes. Water droplets. His air's not clean. He's breathing wet, as divers say; he's got an in-leak, as divers say. But what do divers say about diagnosing this shit when you're crammed inside a sperm whale's throat? He can't reseat his mouthpiece, can't clear the exhaust valve, can't tighten the second-stage diaphragm, none of it.

With the last slam of his head, Jay buries his face into the tissue, a hot, pulsing place to hide. He tastes iron. Whale mucosa. Discovers his lips are parted. He realizes he's about to cry out for Mitt, Dad, Daddy. The agony of his foot, the floppy judder of his pleading limbs, the web of water in his lungs. Cry out, go ahead, let go, give up.

But he doesn't.

Jay thinks of the thoracentesis, the pneumonectomy, words he doesn't understand beyond Mom's gloomy tone and Nan's all-caps emphasis. The chemo. The radiation. The catheter draining yellow curds. Mitt, too, was snagged by fate's teeth. Mitt, too, got swallowed up. But he hung on as long as he could.

Jay can do this.

He's *got* to do this.

For himself.

By himself.

655 PSI

The cramp recedes. You gut them out, they usually do. Jay trains his mouth and tongue to filter as much moisture from his inhales as possible, like drinking through a cracked straw. He thinks the words *helmet jellyfish* as hard as he can until his brain serves up the fact, probably planted by Mitt, that Periphylla will only light up for ten or fifteen seconds at a time. He's just got to reactivate the creature to see how to navigate these last couple feet.

Jay's opposite hand is busy throttling a node of throat tissue. Jay raps his hooded forehead against Periphylla. Head-butting a stinging jellyfish—nothing makes sense anymore.

The jelly goes valentine-red.

BAUM

Jay's extremities tingle. He's not inside a throat. He's inside a heart. The ocean's heart. Mitt's heart. Mom's heart. Nan's and Eva's hearts. All of them together, that's why it's so large.

THROOSH

He's the blood in their veins, pulsing harder, shooting farther.

Jay raises his right knee, wedging it between the throat and his belly, and wiggles his toes to find the next furrow of flesh. Yes. His left foot still throbs but is functional. It, too, finds a toehold. Yes. He shoves his tank backward, pinning himself diagonally like a swallowed toothpick, and explores above with his right hand. Yes. The jellyfish's apple shine helps him find a knob of flesh, an irrelevant malformation to the whale, life itself to Jay. He takes it.

Yes.

Fingers. Biceps. Thighs. Butt. Pull. Heave. Lurch.

He's the blood but also the bile.

630 PSI

Top of the throat.

There, in the jelly's red light: the seal's claw marks.

Jay's muscles spasm as he tries to coalesce scattered thoughts. He's here, the point from which the seal escaped. But how the fuck does he get the mouth open?

He relives the horrors of the whale's mouth.

The necropolis of teeth. The burial pits of the corresponding sockets. The fat, purple, flopping tongue—maybe he can find the root of it? Punch it. Scratch it. Bite it. Take out Beaky, let Beaky give it hell. But no part of the tongue is on this side of the throat. He's going to have to come up with something else.

In the seconds it takes Jay to plot this, Periphylla dies.

Nothing purposeful about it, the dingy dwindle of a flashlight battery's last sigh of power. Jay's cored with loss. Jellyfish breathe via saltwater; it probably died after Jay entered the gullet yet still sloughed off luminous particles, an ally even in death.

Jay longs to watch the jelly's last speck of light fully fade, grave dirt tossed over a real body, not like Mitt's empty Moss Landing plot. But Jay's only got one second to memorize everything he can. He stares ahead, eyes wide behind his mask. Dark magenta flesh in the rough shape of two giant lips, pressed tight, that's it, that's everything.

With one anomaly.

The left third of the throat, right behind the whale's sealed-off mouth, is occupied by a three-foot column of flesh rising at an angle toward a goosebeak-shaped knob.

Then the grave is filled.

Lost in pristine darkness, Jay works to interpret what he saw. It hits him with peristaltic force. The instant he was sucked into the throat's eclipse, he saw and felt this spoutlike column, squishy but firm. He'd even tried to hold on to it before Architeuthis yanked him down. Like the aftermath of a photo flash, Jay still sees a red-hued negative of the goosebeak shape and—yes!—there's a thin gap on the column's left side, too. Which means he should be able to wrap his arms around it.

Jay's muscles sob in relief. Something solid to hold on to!

Then a jolt, a wild spin, and the world's loudest gasp—

—as the whale explodes from the surface of the water.

606 PSI

Humpbacks like to throw their entire bulk from the water, corkscrewing midair, flippers out, every gully of skin ribboning white foam across blue sea before they slap down to their sides, tossing twin tidal waves thirty feet into the air. No one's sure why they do it. To exercise, to remove lice and barnacles, to say hello to other whales. Maybe they do it for fun.

Sperm whales rarely get so much air. Jay was never lucky enough to see a sperm breach up close. But he's seen them in dozens of videos. Their cruiser-sized heads and submarine bodies demolishing placid waters, flippant shows of power from balletic behemoths.

Jay experiences it as weightlessness. The fifty-ton crush of muscle and blubber abruptly gone. He didn't realize how shallow his breathing had become until his rib cage expands, unfolding billows. Oh god, the space, the luxury, the whoosh through his regulator for what feels like an hour. He is with angels, lifted.

The glory is tainted by knowing what comes next.

Jay hurls his left hand at the goosebeak column, ends up punching it. Feels like raw steak wrapped around wrought iron—there's bone in there—but Jay's knuckles, padded by dead jellyfish and old gym sock, are rebuffed unhurt. He rolls sideways with the whale's twist, a two-second midair lob, and slots his hand into the slim left-side gap and hooks his whole arm through it, then locks that arm in place with a right hand to his left wrist—

As the whale crashes down.

2014

Fucking off at church, a header down the stairs, nineteen stitches.

2017

Recess football, full tackle, eighth-grader twice his size, blackout.

2019

Mom pulls out from Gianni's Pizza, driver's-side collision, Jay's head cracks fiberglass.

2022

Swallowed by a whale and chewed by its stomach, if you can believe that shit.

577 PSI

No hit Jay's ever taken comes close. The whale lands on its right side; the entire right half of Jay's body feels pulverized, skin ripped off like wrapping paper, meat clobbered to mush and bones to powder, organs broken like eggs. Despite exploded eardrums, despite the boom of the breach and the landing's locomotive roar, Jay hears things, a wet snap in his neck, a splinter from his ribs like stomped wicker, a woody pop from his hip.

Jay rebounds, gravity's revenge, he's certain his flesh has been hurled from his skeleton and now slurps, squid-like, down the gullet. He's clinging to the fleshy goosebeak, all he knows to do, as the whale floats and bobs, gentle now.

Jay's body's hums hard, a fork tuned to misery.

Sawing through that hum, a rattlesnake hiss.

More memories of wharf rat shenanigans: a kid flashing Jay a photo of the twenty-seven-foot tapeworm-like Placentonema gigantissima, extracted alive from the placenta of a sperm whale and coiled in a jar like an infinite piece of spaghetti. Jay's whale is male, but still he imagines this as the source of the hiss: a monster worm twisting through guts to get him. Why not? What other trial does this whale have left to offer? Then Jay hears the noise a second time and identifies it.

He's heard this sound a hundred times.

Mitt taught his son to identify whales by their blowhole sprays. It's your best shot at knowing who goes there. The vertical geyser of the blue whale. The cheerleader pompoms of the right whale. The bushy plume of the humpback. And the sperm whale's powerful blow, shot forward at a low angle off the tip of the nose.

Jay's body is shattered and radioactive, yet his instinct is the same as any Gardiner Whale Watching ticket holder, to lean his hips against the railing and try to see the spray. That's how he discovers his eyes have been glued shut since the whale flopped itself back into the sea.

He opens them to a goldfish glint.

Jay blinks at the helmet jellyfish. Still dead. Jay looks straight ahead. Light.

It's leaking through the whale's mouth.

552 PSI

A feather of fresh air over Jay's cold skin, blood-crusted nose, grimed cheeks, and cloven, methane-rawed lips refreshes him like spray from a brand-new hotel shower. The whale must be holding a vertical pose, nose pointed skyward, taking the long, easy breaths it's craved since the orca attack. Its mouth and throat remain shut. But light finds a way.

Here in the realm of the sun.

Jay's neck feels padded in a scarf, swelling thick, something wrong, but he strains for the marigold blush anyway, inhales its pollen and tastes its ocean, which hits his desert tongue like effervescent cola amid a rollick of clean ice. It's worth every nerve being gnashed between his vertebrae.

He dangles from the goosebeak column, swaying, drinking it in.

Cliff wind, birdsong, cherry, and chocolate.

So magnificent that Jay, at first, doesn't notice the doubly fantastic.

The sound of people.

523 PSI

For two years Jay broke sweat as an unsalaried swabbie, taking tickets, cleaning toilets, mopping puke, bringing Mitt casks of hot, sugary coffee. He got so he could track the progress of any whale-watching tour by the passenger noises.

The titters of anxious boarding. The whoops as *Sleep* hit stride and skidded over waves. The quizzical timbres when whales were tardy. The elongated yawns when nothing had shown by hour two. The bird-wing gasps and jubilant squeals when a whale breached close, big enough to blot out the sun. It was the awe they'd paid for: a precious few seconds when all senseless toil was forgotten.

That's what Jay hears now.

He holds his breath—safe to do here at the surface—and tries to hear over his heart.

There's a boat. With people. So close, Jay distinguishes different tones: a woman, a man, a Spanish accent, a question, a laugh. Can't be penetrating a solid foot of blubber. Has to be leaking through the whale's mouth or the nasal canal to the blowhole. And if Jay can hear the people, then the people should be able to hear—

"HELP!"

The tight tube of the throat reverberates Jay's cry. His blasted eardrums fizzle. It's the loudest sound he's made since being swallowed— until now, what good was it to yell? Jay spits out his regulator and screams for all he's worth, lips stretching so wide they rip.

"HELP! HELP! HELP!"

His panic panics him. He's panting, sweating, shaking, listening so hard it hurts, and there! There's the people again! They haven't fled, thank god, but Jay doesn't detect concern or confusion in their tones, only delighted chatter.

"I'M INSIDE THE WHALE! HELP ME! HELP ME!"

The whale sprays. The people on the boat applaud.

Jay gags on blood, his throat tilled up by his volume, like he's got his own tiny diver in there raising hell. Other, heavier blood sloshes over him. The whale, too, bleeds from somewhere, through the esophagus, maybe the trachea.

He coughs his mouth clear and looks around, desperate for a brainstorm, but the eke of sunlight only allows the scantest details about his surroundings. Jay feels slippage in his hand-grip, the only thing keeping him from the long drop down.

"What do I do?"

Sperm whales rarely feed on the surface. This mouth is not going to open. Even worse, sperms only spray their blowholes four to eight times before dipping back under. This whale's already sprayed, what? Three times?

"What the fuck do I do?"

Another spray: that's four. More blood, too. The whale could tip over and do its fluke-up any second, and that'll be the game, no matter how far Jay climbed, how hard he fought. He nearly pulled it off by himself, just like he wanted. But that should have never been the goal.

"Dad!"

Outside: boaters gabbing.

"Dad! Please!"

Inside: throat widening as the lungs deflate.

"Dad! Wake up!"

With that, Jay's dams prove to be paper, not brick.

512 PSI

Jay cries.

Like he hasn't since boyhood. He feels wild, out of control. Tears like chips of ice in the heat. He's forgotten the details of crying. How it stuffs up your nose. How acutely the tears sting. He's not just crying, he's sobbing, he's wailing, spraying emotion as if through a blowhole, snorts of putrid air digging into bleeding lungs locked by broken ribs and settled over a broken hip.

Just plain broken.

"Wake up, Dad, I need you!"

(We hear)

(You)

Weak—but that Mitt Gardiner gnar is a life preserver.

"What do I do?"

Until cancer outfoxed him, Mitt could wiggle out of any underwater fix, anywhere, anytime. Whatever's left of the old man inside the whale rises to the challenge, perhaps for the final time.

(What are you holding on to)

500 PSI

Jay takes it as one of Mitt's riddles. He's holding on to a lot. He's holding on to the belief that his sisters will accept him again for having tried to find Mitt's remains. He's holding on to faith that Mom will forgive him for spending his last two years at the hearth and table of someone else's family. He's holding on to the portrait he painted of Mitt in ugly colors, the leisure of disdain, the ego lift in looking in no direction but forward.

He's holding on to hate when he should have held on to hope.

(With your arms Jay)

(What are you holding on to with your arms)

Affection in the voice. A smiling sort of humor. Oh, right: Jay blinks past streaming tears at the hard, gooey column he's hooked his left arm around. Its position at the throat's far left is fucking weird. One thing consistent across all species is bodily symmetry.

But even among whales, the sperm whale is quirky, beyond the blimp head thermosed with spermaceti. Insight tickles Jay from the dark. He's studied so hard for two years: he calls up textbook diagrams of human throats, the big-city intersection of trachea and esophagus.

Another spray: that's five.

"Larynx! This is the larynx!"

Larynx. What even is it? Think, think! The larynx allows air to flow into the lungs and controls the vocal cords of beings that have them. Pick a mammal, any mammal, and the larynx is smack center in the throat. But in a sperm whale? Eccentric, bizarre, an asymmetrical evolution to give it space to swallow giant and colossal squids. But so what? What use is it to Jay besides being an organ he can dangle from until he's dead?

(Listen to your crying)

"I'm going to die!"

(Listen to your sobbing)

"I'm going to die here! Help me!"

(It has always sounded the same to us Jay)

"Help me! Help me!"

(But only now do we truly hear it)

It's not easy. In fact, it's the hardest thing he's ever done, but Jay steels himself and does the same, listening back, as two memories surface and, like bull sperms, butt heads.

2013

"Folks at the top of their fields, type-A take-chargers, you plop them in a dentist chair and suddenly they won't even open up and say ahh, won't move their tongues when you ask them. They're like little babies."

Hewey says it, though, with a laugh. He likes these people. He likes *people*.

"But not your kid, Mitt. He's not afraid of anything I stuck in there."

Jay's eight and proud. One month before Hewey retires from dentistry. Jay got in for a final cleaning two days ago, and he was a champ, didn't flinch, didn't choke, didn't cry. He felt like a Gardiner man. Dad, though, harrumphs. All three are piled into Dad's truck, on the way to someplace Jay won't remember.

"I had a lady in from the aquarium—you'll like this, Mitt. I had to numb her up, she was all nervous. And I pat her hand and ask her what her specialty is, you know, chitchat. And she says cetacean respiration. Huh? Dolphins and whales, she says, how they breathe and whatnot. Tells me she's working on this theory about sperm whales. They talk with clicks, right? But their larynx, they've got a vocal fold for some reason. This lady's theory is that baby sperms actually use them. They move the vocal folds. And just maybe, they cry out for their mommies."

Crying is a sore subject, puts Jay on alert. But Dad doesn't seem to be listening.

"Once they grow up, they stop crying?" Jay asks.

"That's her theory. Adult whales, the fold just sits there, doing squat."

Hewey raises a brow so bushy it brushes the safari hat brim.

"When it could be making the loudest scream in the sea."

2015

"He's ten. Lots of ten-year-olds don't like swallowing pills."

"You think I like diving in landfills? You think I like *any* of the shit-ass work I do to take care of this family?"

Unrelated memory, yet connected, somehow, emphatically. Mom and Dad fighting. Jay's got a lung infection and antibiotics. But he's a mess at swallowing pills, they catch in his throat. Plus this one tastes like tar. He gagged it up twice, eyes watering, before faking a swallow and dropping it in the kitchen trash. Dad didn't buy it. He demanded to know if Jay really swallowed it, and Jay broke down, confessed the whole thing, and now he's got both arms in the trash, feeling past fruit rinds and chicken bones for the tiny pellet, crying.

"Let him up, Mitt. Crying's bad for his infection."

"Not until he finds it. That shit's expensive."

"I know how much it cost. I bought it. With *my* money."

"Oh, great. Humiliate me while you're at it. I'm not good enough because I won't play society's game."

Jay's long, snotty wails ache his ill lungs and rattle silverware in the dish rack. He's too old to cry this hard, he's a crybaby, he hates how it makes Dad hate him.

"You think yelling at him is going to make him any better at swallowing pills?"

"Won't you two shut up?" Door slam, Nan.

"I'd stop worrying about his dainty emotions and start worrying about what happens if he doesn't take his medicine!"

"I hate you! I hate everyone!" Door slam, Eva.

Jay scoops two handfuls of soggy garbage, eyes blurry, chest hitching, all their secret trash laid out in the open.

"I'm so sick of this shit! It is taking the life from my body and killing it!"

"What a terrible thing to say."

"'They had become dull and solvent.'" A quote Jay won't recognize from *Cannery Row* for another two years. "*Dull* and *solvent.*"

"With your children present, Mitt."

Jay touches a pellet. Pulls it out. A piece of corn. Disgusting. He can't take it anymore, his hands dripping with dreck, sick on top of sick, the pill not the only thing lost. He keens, the loudest cry of his life.

"You hear that? That's a baby's cry! Babies cry for their mommy! How about you call me when he decides to grow up?"

475 PSI

(Cry)

Jay knows by now to listen.

He bites into the jellyfish, cold and sour, and rips it from his left hand, and spits it out, down the throat, repeats the same animalistic act with the gym sock. Finally, two hands again—and he grabs the larynx with both of them.

If he can force this whale to produce a sound no human being has ever heard, there's no way those people nearby can ignore it. They'll radio for help, get the coast guard.

Move the vocal fold, Hewey said. But what does that mean? Hewey only had the vaguest idea. Mitt, for all he knew of sea creatures, didn't have this kind of specialized knowledge. As hard as Jay has studied, high school biology terminates at fetal pigs. He's screwed, he's doomed—

(We are not the only ones provided)

"What? What does that—"

(You are not alone)

"I am alone! I am!"

(You have never been alone)

Jay's grappling with the larynx when the meaning unlocks.

Mitt, Jay, Mitt, Jay: the egotism of focusing on the males.

When it's the female pod that typically does the rescuing.

Mom, Zara Gardiner, née Zara Plath. Eva Gardiner, named after the actor. And Nan Gardiner, short for Nancy, seven years Jay's elder, master of science in speech-language pathology from San Diego State, doing speech rehab for stroke patients at a Bakersfield nursing home. Always sounded icky to Jay, but Nan was a barracuda. She chomped onto the profession in high school and never let go.

Thanksgiving 2019, nine months before the *Sleep* debacle, Nan held court in the turkey aftermath, sunglasses stabbed into her hair. She tore a scrap of skin from the carcass and knifed a slit in the center to demonstrate how vocal cords work. Two flaps open and relax for breathing, but cartilage narrows it tighter so it can be vibrated upon exhale. Voilà—sound.

Jay digs his naked heels into the gullet walls, buying time for his free hand to probe the larynx. If Hewey's patient was right and there's a vocal fold, what the fuck does it even feel like? Jay pictures Nan's turkey skin. Probably like that, soft and useless, like earlobes.

The only aberrations he feels are hard, like cartilage.

Hold on, though, isn't that what Nan said? It's cartilage that does the moving. The thyroid, she said; the cricoid. No telling if this oceanic alien has, either. But if the vocal fold exists, it's going to be connected to cartilage.

Jay explores the larynx with his right hand. Squishy tissue, sticky mucus.

He pushes past what feels like elastic, maybe the epiglottis, before abruptly feeling a cannonball of hot air. It's got to be a gale-storm exhale from the whale's trachea. On cue, a blood splash and blowhole blast—seven sprays now, each gorier than the last.

If the science is correct, the whale is due to dip under.

Jay's elbow hurts, hands hurt, ankles hurt. Shoulder tendons knotted as rope. That exhalation: It suggests the vocal fold is nearby, doesn't it? Jay closes his eyes against the pulsing nightmare and focuses every sense into his fingertips. He's got to be meticulous, probe every inch of this organ.

There. Right by Jay's shoulder. Hard nodule beneath the slick tissue. He rubs it in order to understand it. Feels like tire rubber. Roughly the shape of a teacup handle. Handles: they exist to move things. Jay grips it and goddamn if it doesn't move. If this is cartilage, it has to be operating something on its other end, that's the whole point of the stuff.

The vocal fold. It has to be.

Jay's got to get the vocal fold into the canal of exhalation. But it's a machine he has no idea how to run. He pushes the teacup cartilage. It moves. It's the only part of the larynx that does. Jay rolls it toward the mouth. Nothing. Fucking nothing. His hand slips from the mucus. He gasps, bashes about for the handle, five loud slaps, then finds it again and digs in his nails.

This time, Jay pulls the cartilage handle toward the whale's belly.

And hears a low flap—a sail caught in a puff of wind.

What if that's the sound of a vocal fold tented into a trachea?

Jay cranks the handle harder.

"Breathe!"

The gullet narrows as the whale inhales.

"Yes! Exhale! Exhale!"

The whale obeys. Blowhole spray number eight, wet dynamite.

Through larynx, membranes, cartilage, his own hand, Jay feels vibration.

Somewhere, the vocal fold flaps louder, a flag in full gale.

Until a different sound takes over.

If the boaters are champagne types, Jay thinks, their glasses just shattered.

448 PSI

Like a coyote howl, but less manic; like a wolf croon in reverse, not mournful but hopeful, a cry less of earth and fur than air and sand, an arcing siren, high pitch rising higher, nipping the cusp of what Jay's broken eardrums can perceive. Comparisons fail. A thin rubber wheel scribbling over tile? Air squealing from a stretched balloon? Pure, pleading grief this is. Not for the whale itself but for the vexing obstruction in its throat.

The whale is crying.

Same as Jay. An ability recalled after a long time dormant.

The vocal fold buzzes as it hasn't since the goliath was a calf. The hum is violent enough to deaden Jay's fingers and scrunch the marble bag of his swollen wrist. Fresh blood buckets his face, into his wetsuit, around his body. Yet Jay's thrilled because the old whale is thrilled. For a few seconds, a gift: it's young again.

The cry piercing the whale's nasal region stops. Jay's own crying dries out, too. His ears throb, expunge blood, some of it his, most of it not. But he hears what he wants to hear from the surface: *nothing.* The boaters' good times are over. They're in shock at a scream no sperm whale could possibly scream. Human tones drift back, one by one, creeped out, concerned. Maybe they're noticing the blood in the water. They'll report it, fetch the CGs—Jay doesn't hear them do this explicitly, but surely they will!

He laughs—disbelief, triumph—his own vocal folds in vibration.

Doesn't mind this pain, not at all.

Jays regrips the cartilage, still laughing, possibly sobbing.

"Do it again! Exhale again!"

Jay feels the lungs expand once more.

Then: a red flash. Red because Jay's eyes remain pressed shut. So he doesn't get to see sunlight during the swift opening of the whale's mouth. But he hears fish sploosh inward and feels them strike his body, humanlike in combined weight. Jay's grip was shitty to begin with. With arms this strangely twisted, there's really no hope.

Jay slips. Handholds gone.

Food in the throat. Open wide. A muscular, swallowing squeeze.

Jay's shoved back down the gullet.

423 PSI

This time, the hail of water and fish feels like a baptism.

Jay's back in the stomach's first chamber, clasped in muscle, suffused in rotting stench. His legs. They're broken. Broken so bad they don't even feel like legs, more like strange refuse the whale gulped up along with all the plastic bags. Half of him is dead weight. He won't be climbing again. He won't be going anywhere.

From down here, he can't hear any of the people.

He's alone. Again, again, again.

There's a convulsion of loss, naturally. Disappointment, of course. But no blame, no blame at all. What Mitt said before still holds true.

(*A whale eats when a whale eats*)

Jay finds himself awash in strange serenity. Could be the shock of two broken legs. Could be his dwindling air. Could be brain damage. Or could be he's feeling what all souls near the end have no choice but to feel. Acceptance of foregone fate. Gratitude for being gifted existence, if only a sliver.

If the whale is truly Mitt, it is also Squid, Shark, Skate, Lobster, Crab, Shrimp, Krill, Sponge, Starfish, Jellyfish.

And Jay—it will be Jay, too.

He once saw a TV special of a sperm whale dissection, Mitt calling out the highlights. The scientist pulled back seven inches of blubber to reveal a hidden echolocational organ called the *museau de singe*, the "monkey's muzzle," which looked exactly like the lips of a monkey.

Jay suspects the whale's collected spirits go beyond only animals it consumes. Maybe he'll dig around down here, see what else he finds. Elephant tusk. Rabbit ear. Turkey feather. Salamander tail. Ostrich leg. Butterfly wing.

That's the baptism: initiation into a ghost menagerie, extinction canceled.

Now, a kind of peace. Not the peace of the whale's dive, that skull-swollen, psychotropic bliss. The peace Discalced Carmelite nuns find in skinning God from Son from Holy Spirit. The peace parishioners feel after consuming the body and blood of Christ. What always felt brutal to Jay about the natural world now feels like its most elegant design.

We all eat each other, like Hewey said.

That's why we live forever.

392 PSI

Frail peristaltic waves squeeze the fish—not bioluminescent, just regular joes—into the next chamber. It doesn't even hurt. Jay goes fetal, comfiest pose for his final cradle. The whale will bleed out soon. If eaters don't annihilate it instantly, the whale's carcass—and Jay's carcass inside it—will sink quietly through the fathoms, all six and a half thousand feet of Monterey Canyon, before gentling onto the sea bottom, soft and pliable from its own putrefying gases.

Every scorching wound in Jay's body cools as he fancies it.

Scientists call it a *whale fall*.

Outshouted by class units on whale song and clockwork readings of Steinbeck was a more beautiful lesson. A single dead whale nurtures its deep-sea landing spot for ages. Creatures of mind-boggling anatomy, ignorant of the concept of light, come to feed. Rattails. Hagfish. Isopods. They tunnel and gnaw and lick and suck and absorb until the fatty colossus is nothing but methane bubbles, spilled oil, and bone.

Life doesn't stop there. Bacteria gobble up the fat inside whale bones. This makes hydrogen sulfide. Which powers microbes. Soon the bones vanish beneath glittering carpets of worms, glowing bacterial mats of clams, mussels, snails, limpets. Hundreds of species over decades, centuries. At last the bones are so nibbled away they create something like a coral reef—an entire new ecosystem of life.

Sermons call this communion.

Jay smiles, curls tighter. Dying here is so much better than dying on land, where his pale, smelly corpse would be dressed and perfumed only to be mooned at by mourners out to avoid similar fates, before being plugged into overpriced soil, from which his best hope for immortality would be fossilization: a stone in a future museum, propped alongside other long-dead curiosities.

No, thank you. One ticket for the whale watching.

He is awed. Will be a figure of awe. A son, a brother, a father.

363 PSI

(We are sorry you did not get out)

Mitt's faltering voice, captive to the whale's fading body.

Jay's nod ripples stomach sludge.

"It's okay."

(We are weak)

"It's okay, Dad."

(We will die soon)

"Dad. Dad. Shh."

Shh: Mitt had shushed Jay hundreds of times in the days before Jay realized how his childlike blabber spoiled his dad's quiet idylls. On a beach, Mitt listening to the oceans for hours. On a boat, Hewey fishing, Mitt enraptured by waves, only waves. Underwater, Jay darting from rock to rock, critter to critter, while Mitt burned half his tank studying a single tree of kelp. How was the world "dull and solvent," but Mitt's lingering inactivity wasn't?

Jay gets it now. All the things he hoped to learn after graduating and leaving Monterey, the degree at Berkeley, the job at Yellowstone, it's all here. The infinite inside the infinitesimal.

Look at the stomach. Really look at it. See the wagon trails traced through vessels and fat. See Jupiter's storms. Valleys of fire. Collapsing constellations. A million teardrops. Paths through forests. Dinosaurs, future dinosaurs. A yellow crescent moon. Men, women, snakes. Kissing lips. The silver ritual of rings. Bunches of pink balloons. The curve of a lover's back. Baby chub. Elderly wrinkles. Cracked continents. The wrong road. A flood. Things drowned and ascended. Snowfall. A tree to climb. Spiderwebs. Solar flares.

Shh. See it?

332 PSI

The last of the bioluminescence winks out.

Jay, blind now, closes his eyes, velveting the black, and pats a hand along his BCD until he finds the suicide clip. Slowly, he detaches it. He thumbs the spring-loaded retaining gate inward, isolating the hook. He presses it into his thumb pad. Might be pointy enough to live up to its nickname. He could pierce his jugular. He'll have to remove his hood, though, have to peel the neoprene bandage from his neck. It all seems so difficult.

He thinks of what Hewey said about Jesus and suicide. He thinks of the Carmelite Monastery. He thinks of the whale proportions of the sanctuary's rib cage. He lets the suicide clip drop, into the gunk, gone.

"Maybe we. Should pray."

(Too late)

(To start now)

Both their voices slowing.

"The Bible's got. A story for everything."

(Steinbeck is better than God)

"Come on. You only read *Cannery Row*."

(You only read Cannery Row)

"Okay. Hit me. With some Steinbeck."

(Steinbeck trained as a)

(Marine biologist)

"A-ha. So that's why. You dig him. I remember one part. Of the book. Where the guy. The main guy. He collects starfish. He's pulling them out of a bag. And starfish like to cling to stuff. But there's nothing to cling to. So they cling to each other. So tight they get all knotted up. That was neat. To imagine."

(All of our so-called successful men are sick men)

"Huh?"

(You wanted a verse)

"Oh. Right."

(There's more)

"Go ahead."

(All of our so-called successful men are sick men with bad stomachs and bad souls)

"Stomachs, huh? That's pretty good."

(Of course it is good)

(It is Steinbeck)

"You know what. Part I liked?"

(We are happy you liked it)

"*Part*, I said. One *part*. When the prostitutes. Made a quilt. From lingerie."

(We used to like that part too)

Jay will never know lingerie's sheer silk. But the stomach lining isn't so bad.

(We should have asked what your favorite part was)

(We are sorry we never asked questions)

(We wanted to know but were afraid)

"Of what?"

(Answers to questions have weight)

(And we wanted to stay light)

(We are sorry)

"We got a. Few minutes left. What do you want to know?"

Not just the voice. The heart, the pulse, the lungs, all slower.

(Do you have a girlfriend)

"No."

(Do you have a boyfriend)

"I appreciate. That. But's it's hard. The pandemic."

(What did you want to be when you grew up)

"Something with nature. Park ranger. Something."

(Did you ever want a dog)

Jay laughs. Feels good despite punctured lungs.

"Weirdo."

(We always felt bad you kids never had a dog)

"Don't sweat it. The least of our problems."

(What did you hope to accomplish)

"To do something. That people got some good out of."

(You would have done it)

"Thanks."

There will be no girlfriend, no boyfriend, no career, no mark made on the world. That doesn't change how Jay feels here and now. The simple sharing of hope, its weight not so heavy after all, is a wonder. A lifting. A rising.

A surfacing.

301 PSI

Thump. Thump.

It's comparable to the nudges of the sperm whale pod. Jay is lightly bounced within the digestive hammock. The whale bobs, up and down. Waves, steeper than any Jay's felt until now. One explanation, maybe. The whale has sailed into the sandy shallows and the thumps are its underside touching the floor with the bottoming of every wave.

Fits everything Jay knows. Whales in distress often head for the coast, swim parallel to the beach, even belly up to the sandbar, where strength normally reserved for swimming can be applied to breathing. Shallows are warmer, too, freeing up the energy whales earmark for regulating temperature. There's a danger of beaching. Jay hopes it doesn't happen.

If any whale deserves a whale fall, it's this one.

The stomach's shiver feels like sobbing shoulders. Jay strokes the quivering tissue.

"It's okay. Don't fight it."

He's at Dad's bedside now. Finally, he got here.

Jay feels Mom behind him, Nan, Eva, Hewey. He has a funny thought. No one carries the best parts of themselves. The best parts are those held inside of others.

"Let go, Dad."

The whale's skeleton groans, an old barn against a storm. Erratic rhythms as the whale's organs quit playing in harmony. Jay's aware of the cold stink of blood, the oily shrug as it coagulates atop the sludge. Far above, the blowhole. No more screaming. The blowhole gasps, gasps, gasps.

(Jay)

"Don't talk."

(Jay we)

"Whatever it is, I understand."

(We want you to escape us)

"Dad. Dad, I can't."

(I want you to escape me)

Jay shakes his head, hood zipping across blood-slicked stomach.

But he can't unhear what the voice just said.

Jay gasps. The blowhole gasps, too, as if father and son have joint control.

Lungs near empty.

But hearts. Hearts full.

(I always wanted you to escape me)

(Only I forgot I forgot I forgot)

2005

"My son."

A man's face. Big as the moon. Eyes gray craters. Scars the eroded riverbeds of bygone waters. Gravitational pull: Jay wants to be with this face forever. Jay's swaying. Not in a whale stomach. He's being rocked in the crook of an arm. Jay tastes salt. Not a whale's ingested seawater. It's tears dropping from the man's face.

The man is his daddy.

Jay is one month old.

No, he's just low on oxygen. Has blood on the brain. None of this is real.

But what *is* real? There's what we have seen, heard, smelled, tasted, touched. Then there's what we know in every platelet to be truth. Jay is newborn, this giant is his father, and if he can't believe in that, he can believe in that ceiling crack he's seen a billion times before. The brown-sugar smell of baby toys. The background yap of his sisters. The dishes clattering in the sink. The pinch of diapers. This is home.

Dad whispers. Tears keep dropping. The last tears Jay will ever see from him.

"I'm not worth you."

Jay's soft larynx can't form words. But his thoughts are as old as the ocean.

(Yes you are Daddy)

"I'm going to screw you up."

(Of course you are Daddy)

"But maybe I can teach you things."

(I am sure you will Daddy)

"So one day you can live the life you want. Anything you want."

(Why are you in such a hurry Daddy)

"I'll make sure of that. I'll give you all the tools."

(I do not want tools Daddy)

"So when it matters, Son, you'll know what to do."

(Daddy all I want is you)

274 PSI

Jay opens his eyes to steamy velour black. But he's grown a mystical second set of eyes and sees the gut in its former phosphorous green. Each glowing speck a bright intelligence gathered to witness this freak of biology, this evolutionary crawl: a stomach that is also a womb.

It is ready to deliver.

"Dad . . ."

(Live)

"Are you sure?"

((Live))

"Maybe there's another way."

(((Live)))

"Give me a chance to think!"

((((LIVE))))

Mitt's law still holds sway. Jay's every nerve ending sparks. Which quickens breathing. Which eats more oxygen. His cylinder slithers air, so thin now Jay smells, or imagines he smells, that other thing. The slinking, lurking smell so pervasive he hasn't given it one thought since exiting the stomach's second chamber.

The smell of Sheol Landfill.

Methane.

The whale's stomach is full of methane.

What had Mitt said while Jay dangled from the larynx?

(You have never been alone)

Nan helped Jay in the throat. Now it was Jay's other sister, the over-shadowed Eva, one year out of college and doing equipment tests at a San Jose bio lab after studying chemical engineering at UC Irvine, a degree enlivened by bizarro experiments she reproduced like magic tricks during visits home. Basic household items, ladies and germs, whole milk plus vinegar plus paper towels plus microwave equals polymer plastic, ain't that neat?

Eva taught Jay just what he needs to know.

He shifts his arms. They didn't expect to ever move again, and they're pissed, broken bones gristling, joints mewling. Jay plunges his hands into the sludge. Amid the tarrying fish, the krill, the crustaceans, he sorts the familiar lineup. Diving fin. Concrete. Gym sock. Plastic bags.

Cardboard box.

In the fantasy light cascade, Jay reads the box as easily as he did originally. Flattened. Weathered. Faded red. A scuffed illustration of pots and pans. Big letters: *BRILLO*. Smaller letters: *More Soap, Longer Lasting! Lemon Fresh Scent!* Smaller still: *10 Steel Wool Soap Pads*.

Hard to think, heaving, regulator hissing like coffee dripped to the burner, he checks the console, lousy news, 274 psi, deep into danger. That is, if the console hasn't already been busted by the onslaughts that have busted him. Enough of that, think: in the folds of Jay's brain lies a lesson from chemistry class, survival manuals, playground kids greedy for destruction.

Steel wool is kindling. For a specific kind of spark.

Jay rewinds. Views his whole morning in speedy reverse. Falling upward toward the larynx. The whale shooting tail-first into the depths. Orcas neatly replacing stolen meat. Eardrums reglued. Hand unstabbed by Beaky. In and out of the second chamber's volcano. The Architeuthis fight more like a parting hug. Feet-first up the gullet. Bounding from the whale's mouth up the canyonside, the silt scattered while searching for Mitt's bones suctioned back into place. Paddling the wrong way through Monastery Beach's danger zone. A backward trek down Carmel Meadows Trail. Driving in reverse to the Tarshish place. Inverted maze through the house, the kitchen, a closed drawer springing open.

Stop. There.

Jay filled his BCD pockets with batteries.

D batteries, mostly, to make up the five pounds he couldn't scrounge up in dive weights. Came up short, though, and chucked in a few random others. Later, beset by fifty whale teeth, Jay flung the batteries into the sea along with his weights. But batteries are small and pesky. Before scaling the gullet, Jay rustled for more, found them, tossed them.

Jay squirrels his hand into his BCD pocket. Feels around.

Nothing. Empty.

His hopes, too, emptied. Wait. Hang on. Something. His numb, acid-burned fingers barely feel it. He cups the object like an injured wren. He draws it out, holds it close, caresses its eight corners until he's sure of what it is.

A single 9-volt battery.

Bridged by steel wool, the two knobs of a 9-volt would complete a circuit. A circuit creates a spark. And what can a single spark do? Eva asked. Her eyes feline with the intoxication of catastrophe. City streets ruptured by underground gas pipes. Coal mines steepled in white fire. Apartment complexes turned to gray ash by gas leak combustions. Even an urban legend, a colonoscopy methane blast, some poor dude's ass blown wide open. Spooky because there's a trace of truth.

Methane is flammable. Even explosive.

Mitt said it himself, drunk from the deck of *Sleep*.

Sky-high, Jay. Blow. It. Up.

243 PSI

Jay molds his spine against the gullet's gored sphincter. He tucks the 9-volt under his chin so both hands can pry open the squashed Brillo box. The old glue's stubborn. He tries to knife a finger between the flaps but his hand's wobbly, up, down, all over. He gasps along to every miss.

"Fuck!"

He pulls out his regulator, mouthful of methane like swishing kerosene, and slots the cardboard between his jaws. One of his teeth bends. If Jay bites, the tooth will snap off. He bites. The tooth is history, one more bone chipped, one more splurt of blood, but who cares, he's whipping the box with his jaws like a dog with a rabbit.

It rips open.

Regulator back in. Gasp, gasp—the blowhole echoes in sympathy— gasp, gasp. Jay peels open the box. It's packed with flat discs. Probably silver, the lemon-yellow soap bled out long ago. Jay grabs one steel wool pad and drops the rest. With his other hand, he knuckles the 9-volt from under his chin. He holds them next to each other, two halves of a circuit.

(No Jay)

"I—have to—can't hardly—breathe—"

((((THINK JAY))))

Eva's back, eyes bright enough for Jay to see them through her sunglasses as she describes factories enflamed, streets cleaved, the apocryphal colonoscopy. It's not fire Jay has to shield himself from. The Henderson's close to fire resistant and ought to save most of his skin.

It's the blast force that will kill him.

A gas explosion in a space this small? It'll liquidate every organ in Jay's body.

He's got to think like Eva. Like coal miners boring safety vents.

Confining the blast. It's why terrorists use pressure cookers. The problem is the whale's a pressure cooker inside a pressure cooker: a blast in the stomach will never make it to the blubber with sufficient strength. Jay's got to get methane outside the stomach and into the whale's body cavity. That's where the spark needs to heat the methane and explode. Combined with the whale's orca damage, it might just rip apart everything Jay needs ripped.

He palms the Brillo pad, places the 9-volt back into one BCD pocket, and reaches into the other. There: the ruthless yet graceful brutality that fits his hand so shockingly well.

Jay's glad Mitt never let him carry a diving knife.

Beaky is so much better.

211 PSI

No gym-sock cushion this time, no waiting for the perfect peristaltic squeeze. Jay stabs the stomach, a horror flick slasher, a final frenzy he didn't think he had in him.

The first dozen stabs are fruitless, like stabbing a sweater, the stomach fibers easily tolerating Beaky's blade. With every thrust, the back of the beak bores into the hole in Jay's right palm. He feels the wound yawn wider. A few more stabs and the hand will be all hole, his fingers popping off. So what? Jay will just spike Beaky into his wrist stump and keep going.

Suddenly the beak snags as hard as a suicide clip, maybe a lucky strike into a pitted ulcer. Maybe the whale itself shifted its torso to help Jay's aim land true. Though he can't see shit, he feels the pooched lip of a fresh gouge.

Or thinks he feels it. Air supply thready, reality gone misty.

Jay knows this beak so well. Adjusts his grip and now he's sawing. He feels the stagger of stomach tissue starting to tear, but more reliable than that, he hears it, hoarse and wet, like roadkill peeled off pavement. His arm muscles grind, grind until they sag, useless, then his shoulder muscles take over and employ his arms like cheap tools.

He's cut through the stomach, all right. New stench infiltrates his mask, the signature of whatever organ is closest, could be spleen, could be liver, Jay doesn't know what direction he's facing. If odor's rolling in, then methane is rolling out, filling the cavity, putting the fuel for the fire where it needs to be.

Still sawing with his right hand, Jay makes a left-hand fist over the Brillo pad and punches through the gash, then rolls his arm all around. The stomach hole doubles in size and so does the stink, a popped balloon of foul heat, sticky moisture, all the blood and fluid released during the orca attack, everything slippery.

His hands slippery, too—

And Beaky squirts from his palm, through the hole.

"No! Beaky!"

Jay plunges his right arm through the gap, all the way to his shoulder, elbow sinking into something squishy, hand bashing past what feels like slimy grapes, rotten cabbage, a palpitating organ the texture of black banana peel. But no sharp points, no hard curves, nothing that fits in his hand like it was born there.

"Beaky! Come back!"

But his companion, his savior, his good-luck charm, his best friend, it's lost inside the whale, gone forever. Tears pop to Jay's eyes and don't wait, they stream, all the moisture in his body gushing like some critical supply source has been ruptured. He collapses against the side of the stomach, arm still hanging inside the body cavity, and sobs, and sobs, how stupid, how juvenile, but his whole world has shrunk to bedroll size and every loss hurts. If Jay survives, he won't let any bastard tell him that Beaky wasn't real, that Beaky didn't matter. Just because Beaky's remains are lost doesn't mean he didn't earn Jay's grief.

184 PSI

He drags his arm back inside. Right hand so desperately empty. His left hand, though, isn't empty at all. He opens it, feels the scratchy fluff of steel wool.

Jay's right hand is obliterated from the stabbing. Its weight is all off, like the palm meat is gone, the exposed bones cracked, the fingers jiggling by fibrils of skin. He's glad he can't see it. Still has to use it, though. With as much caution as he dares while still moving fast, Jay dips his mangled paw into his BCD pocket. Tries to work the fingers. There's just enough cohesion to pinch and hold.

He brings back out the 9-volt battery.

It's time. Jay's terrified.

He lived his life amid a flood. Mistook drowning as sleeping. The whale was the ark he needed: prison, school, church, sickbed, crib.

When Mitt spoke of old whalers, he clucked over the irony of whale blubber boiled over fires fed with scraps from the same beast: the whale fueled its own destruction.

Now Mitt, one with the whale, was doing the same. Over how many years, even decades, has the beast patiently collected every item Jay Gardiner would one day need? How far ahead do angels of the deep track the collision courses of terrestrial bodies? If there was any way for Jay to return the gift, he would. All he can do is thank them. If only he had the breath.

149 PSI

((((T HIN K))))

Jay's air's low. He's dying. So's the whale.

((((T HI K))))

Think? What's left? More to the point, who's left? Nan and Eva did their best.

((((T I K))))

Yes. Of course.

Mom: who's never, after all, been farther away than the other side of town, who calls Jay all the time, who has rung the Tarshishes once a week for two years to double-check that there's nothing Jay needs that she could give. That memory of Mitt trying to soothe nine-year-old Jay as he cried about flunking school? That was only the story's start.

Next day, Mom drove Jay to school early, spoke with Jay's teacher while rubbing the back of Jay's neck, collected every bit of homework backlog, and that night, with popcorn and root beer, they plowed through the stack together, Jay emerging with a clean slate and a loving awe.

One of the fill-in-the-blank questions they did that night, Jay still knows it. Mom turned it into a seven-word singsong.

Blank plus blank plus blank equals fire.

Jay concentrates, rasping breath, wheezing tank.

Fuel plus blank plus blank equals fire.

He's dropping both battery and steel wool. He's ripping at his BCD.

Fuel plus *heat* plus blank equals fire.

He's taking off his BCD. Why. Why is he doing it.

Fuel plus heat plus *oxygen* equals fire.

Jay believed it impossible to remove his BCD in so cramped a space, but look, with Mom's help he can accomplish anything. Velcro snarl, buckle chime, rubber rip, Jay's shoulder dislocating with a luscious scrunch.

Fuel: methane. Heat: steel wool. Oxygen . . . where?

Only one place.

The BCD is off and Jay is a weightless feather, might float right up the gullet. He rolls the Oceanic onto his hip. Feels like holding a ghost. A shed skin. A body that used to be Jay Gardiner. What fingers he has left read the cylinder's Braille, the steel scripture of the manufacturer, serial number, test date. Mitt can have his Steinbeck; Hewey can have his Torah, Qur'an, New Testicle. Jay will take the Gospel of Faber 120.

Jay tilts the BCD. The console swings, its glow-in-the-dark face a firefly in the night, the SPG dial the final oath of an unwelcome prophet: *149 psi.*

He guides the cylinder valve to the rough, weeping hole Beaky cut through the stomach. The hose connecting the tank to the regulator in Jay's mouth pulls hard, ousting more of his broken teeth. No more breathing wet: he's parched, tongue chasing whatever dervishes of air still circle the tank.

Jay's last inhale is long, sandpapery, excruciating.

Yet wonderful. Fruit juice. Alpine breeze. Dog fur. His lungs inflate and every broken bronchiole, every stabbing rib, every neighboring catastrophe blinks out like snuffed candles, and Jay sits in their ashes, wetsuit arid as sackcloth, conscience clear, mouth quiet.

He holds that breath.

Holds everything.

Regulator futile now, he spits it, grips the chunky plastic handle that screws his octopus retainer to the tank, rolls it counterclockwise. Bones crackle in his wrist. All this time in the whale, all that struggle, and all it takes is a few cranks and his lifeline is gone. Jay pulls the entire set of hoses from the cylinder and pitches it aside.

The K valve is all that's left on the tank, already in the on position. The last precious eddies of air flow from the O-ring, through the stomach's hole, and mix with methane in the whale's abdomen.

At least that's what Jay hopes is happening, holding his breath for life now, ten seconds in, neck tight. With his left hand, he picks up the 9-volt and steel wool, harmless together without oxygen, brings them toward the stomach hole.

And stops.

Which hand should he sacrifice? If the explosion works, the hand cradling the steel wool will be blown to pieces. He's right-handed: protect his right hand. But his right hand is already pulverized and might be a lost cause—if only he could see it, he'd know! Held breath at fifteen seconds, twenty, low burn at his sternum, not fair he has to make this choice, not fucking fair, but Mom's not here to help him, he's got to choose the sacrifice, now, now.

If he lives, he'll have his whole life to become a leftie.

Jay swaps hands, his gored right palm the offering plate, the exposed muscles pricked by the Brillo pad's wires. Last-second fears pummel his brain. Will this work with wet steel wool? What about wet batteries? No time: he reaches his right hand through the hole, into the body cavity, and into the flow of the Faber 120 tank's sympathetic sigh.

2020

Blood-faced, bent-kneed, the last thing Dad said before *You got soft lungs.*

"The second you harpooned a whale, you threw yourself to the boat floor. Like so. You prayed to the tuurngaq your line would hold. Come on, Jay. Pray with me. You like to pray, don't you?"

143 PSI

Jay decides he does.

He presses himself to the boat floor, the whale's belly, only his right hand outside the stomach.

So he doesn't see the gray steel wool go bright red as the 9-volt sets it ablaze. He feels it, though, a cherry bomb of heat, and smells it, smoky iron with a hint of *Lemon Fresh Scent!*, and though he's welded his eyes shut, his eyelids flash orange like—what?—like bright apricot—no, too gentle—golden wheat, no, but closer—butterfly wings, their flutter captures the film-strip speed of it—tiger stripes, goldfish, the honeycombed eyes of a fly—as it divides up the hour of the pearl.

The sound is a single heartbeat magnitudes beyond the whale's *BAUM*. Jay hears it for one instant before his demolished eardrums straight up quit and all that's left is a softer note, a word, not shouted for once but whispered.

(Live)

1965

What has been provided?

1970

What has been provided?

1998

What has been provided?

2000

What has been provided?

2005

Jay is born. For the very first time.

0

He's nowhere. Suspended. Upside down. Maybe dead. No stomach. No second stomach. No gullet. No teeth. No tongue. No mouth. Ideas of flesh no longer organized into principles. He tries moving his limbs to see if he has them. Inconclusive. He tries opening his eyes to see if they still exist.

There is light.

Sun. Nothing like it. Strawberry shine, dawdling honey. Not flat against Jay's skin but creeping soft and heavy. He reaches for it, which tells him he's got an arm, at least one arm, and this activates his back, what he hopes might be his back. Yes, there's a spinal uncoiling, he's got a spine, incredible news.

He tries to smell and, wow, is there smell, he's submerged in thick, meaty odors that push through his teeth—he has teeth—like caramel, before it starts filling his throat. Jay gags—he has a neck, a chest—and the jolt awakes other parts. He's got a stomach. He's got a leg, maybe two.

Jay realizes he can't hear anything only when he begins to hear something: bassy warbles slivering through a drumming silence. The sounds are inside out, capsized, yet he classifies them without effort. That fizz is ocean tide. Those squawks are gulls. Those gobbles come from people.

People.

The people shout. He'd like to shout back. He may even remember how to speak without regulator plastic. But he can't breathe. Why can't he? He discovers he has lips; he opens them, he gives it a try.

A hot, slick surface sucks solid to his lips. Airway blocked. Jay shakes his head—he has a whole head, his neck cracking—he has a neck, and inside it is a brain—a brain, all his. His lips, though, slip from one damp thing to the next. He's close to air, swallows a few bubbles of it, there's sun so there has to be more, but he's going to suffocate all over again if he can't find it fast.

0

Hands, feet, whatever he's got, he drives with any muscle that works, wounds spewing liquid, bones clacking. He's the Placentonema gigantissima, the colossal worm, squirming his face across rippled muscle, cooler sponges of blubber, burning seepage, hot spray, gases like physical things.

Sunlight scarlet through curtains of bloody gel. Cackling fishermen used to say it: nothing bleeds like a liver. Jay's scheme worked—he blew a hole in the whale—and he raises his head as if that's all it takes to emerge. His scalp butts something hard. He's dungeoned. Still no air. Sixty tons of sperm whale have been rearranged and there's no stomach to protect him now. If the wrong organ topples, the backbone collapses, anything, Jay will be crushed.

Artillery blasts: boots stomping through ocean waves. The eek of oars in rowlocks, people congregating, navigating a bay of loose guts, so close their shouts are shrill and dry. Other sounds, too, a repeated, resounding *thwak*, like echoes of the bomb he set off, but fresher, crisper, better.

Almost as good as air.

Jay's hand is caught in a web of clingy tissue, foot trapped in the jack-o'-lantern of a ruptured organ. He's screeching now, chest hiccupping, he's inhaling blood instead of air, it's clotting his throat. Other blood, though, is drying sticky to his face, which tells him there's wind, but where the fuck is it?

He squints through crimson light and finds none of those candy colors they label organs within biology textbooks: "lungs" in lilac, "kidney" a gingerbread brown, "intestines" a bubble gum pink. It's all red, the whale's gobbets masquerading as random items plucked from a dumpster. Bloody shelving, bloody blouses, bloody cymbals, bloody catcher's mitts, a bed of bloody, deflating balloons. Jay's hallucinating because he's dying, he's Mitt at Sheol Landfill, diving toward hell.

0

Dribbles of air, coughing through perforated lungs, gagging, and crawling, the only thing he knows how to do, the thing he's going to die doing. Under a diaphragm serrated into palm fronds, over a hill of blubber but beneath sagging tents of skin, all moving with the sway of surf. Breeze harder, sun hotter, people louder. There's someone in here, can't you tell I'm in here?

They're begging for him.

So are the *thwak* noises, *thwak, thwak, thwak.*

Oxygen gone, pulse skipping, brain cells going dark.

Jay's face sinks into a wall of meat.

Every part of the whale he's touched since explosion has been fractured, erupted, tattered, shaved, severed, jellied, liquified. Except this.

The whale's heart.

Twice the size of Jay, three hundred leathery pounds of quivering muscle and a twitching tapestry of veins. A boulder in Jay's escape path, immovable, the final word. Doesn't matter how many people have come, they'll never find him behind the heart.

Jay stretches his arms around as much of it as he can.

He embraces the heart.

He feels his last bead of air roll from his throat. He doesn't mind. He lets it go with a kiss, his cold, broken lips meeting the heart's hot pulsations. At the end, all the clichés are true. Flayed of its tough skin, insecurities, and regrets, the heart is love. Jay bleeds it right back.

A whisper.

Like foam blown off a wave.

Jay listens. A pinch of confusion. Not what he wants to feel in his final seconds of life. Swift, then, and thunderous, a collision of tides, the scoldings from Mom, Nan, and Eva, in person at In-N-Out Burger, via phone, email, and text, duplicating Mitt's dying plea, *Don't break my heart, don't break my heart, don't break my heart.*

Dad's whisper, at last, gives Jay permission to do the opposite.

(Break it)

0

For his father, his mother, his sisters, he does. Jay shovels his face at the heart, his mouth his widest wound, and bites and chews and rips like a dog. His hands sharpen into trowels, stabbing, digging, gouging seams along artery trails and opening them, his arm shot through the gap, then his shoulder, other arm, head. Inside a tabernacle of flesh, dunked in scalding blood, teeth gnashing rubbery valves, hands finding atriums to sunder. He gathers blood vessels like flowers, unstitches them from pulmonary cloth. Jay's wholly inside now, one leg kicking into this ventricle, one leg into that. His left hand hacks through muscle and is tickled by whiskers of sun. Jay pushes his own heart, rabbity engine, against the cardiac wall, and it's heartbeat against heartbeat, click to click, Jay transmitting codas of his own at last, and he knows, wherever they are, the people he loves receive them: Mom sitting up straight from morning tea, Nan moved to unexplainable tears at her workplace, Eva opening her eyes from oversleep with not her father's name on her lips but her brother's.

0

(Where are you)

The right answer was so simple, Jay had fought it.

Ayekah. Hineini.

I am here.

0

From another dimension, a hand takes Jay's wrist. And pulls. Jay slides forward but his shoulder thuds meat, skull thuds meat, he's the skinniest kid his age and still carries too much body for so small a passageway. Butcher noises reply, wet smacks, the chunky punch of hacking steel, followed by another jolt of motion.

Sunlight bathes Jay's face, warm, clean.

Wind blows through every wound, cool, cotton, perfect.

But being born is scary no matter how many times you do it. Jay screams, the first breath the hardest. His heart shocks itself, triple beat, lava veins, pulse in barraging volleys. He lifts eyelids burdened with goop and feels the weight of blood on his face, at last the painted warrior Dad wanted. Part human, part whale, Jay's being delivered right there in the shallows, blinking up at a team of anxious doctors, what else is new? His second birth is no improvement on his first. Instead of scalpels and forceps, these docs use knives and saws.

Everyone in motion through hip-deep waves. Jay's heavy eyes can't follow. But his burst eardrums do okay. Whale guts, squelching. The ocean's thrush and crash. The *thwak* noises, a church organ full of them now, some kind of drumbeat festivity. Everyone talks over everyone.

Move that blubber, quick.

Clear out those broken teeth, he'll choke.

Barotrauma risk, get oxygen, find us a hyperbaric chamber.

His hand's gone, Jesus.

Burns over most his skin, bleeding from the ears, let's move.

Easy with his neck, those legs.

Ribs poking through the wetsuit there, watch your hands.

His right side's all busted, tip him to his left, his left.

Keep pressure on that neoprene, there's a huge wound under there.

Did he bandage that himself? How the hell is this guy alive?

Jay's body is being handled. They try to steady his neck, but his jaw gets jostled and his head lolls to the side. Facing the ocean. White chaos. Earth's most extravagant fountain. Silos of water blowing fifty feet into the air. The sound like Fourth of July on the beach with Mom.

Whales. More than Jay's ever seen, in photos, in videos, in legend. Could be the pod that escorted Jay's whale to the surface, but probably no relation besides the broader heritage of cetaceans, of leviathans, of angels. Dad once said roughly three hundred thousand sperm whales exist; this must be all of them. Between blowhole sprays of supernatural altitude, a dozen whales roll from the blue; two dozen leap, a black cosmos of crescent planets; three dozen hang midair, having mastered proper flight. Flukes as big as islands smash the sea. It's applause, relief, a crowd of midwives cheering the transfer of life from one beast to the next.

THWAKTHWAKTHWAKTHWAKTHWAK!

Jay feels spray from their flukes.

The water washes crusted blood from his face.

He's able to open his eyes all the way, his nostrils, his mouth.

As his torso is freed from whale parts, Jay's head is jostled in the opposite direction. Will you look at that? The whale didn't park itself at China Cove or Fanshell Beach. Thirty feet away is Monastery Beach—good old Mortuary Beach—that virile arc of golden sand, the Carmelite Monastery peeking from the lush green hills, the world having advanced a dull ninety minutes while Jay lived and died and lived again in the deep.

There's a sperm whale on the beach. Not Jay's whale. A different one, smaller, dead. It's perplexing for only a moment. This is why there was no parking on Highway 1. This is why there is a crowd at this end of the beach. Why there are banks of lights, why there's a bulldozer.

Before Jay arrived this morning, probably last night, a whale beached and died. Scientists descended like ants: it's what scientists do. There's no way to study a whale's physiology but to perform a necropsy on a corpse before it must be buried, or dismembered and trucked to landfills, or towed out to sea, the best option: a second chance at whale fall.

Jay asked his dad why whales beach. But no one knows. Could be their echolocation is bedeviled by submarine sonar. Could be chemical pollution. Solar storms. Toxic algae. Ear parasites. A rise in orca predation. Could be climate change or something beyond our comprehension: a protest against what we have done to their world.

So much hubbub over one death. Dad, in his cancer months, would have scorned such attention. Jay feels certain the beached whale will get its whale fall. A single life is nothing but a spark. The explosion is everything *after* death, the generations of reverberation. Every consumed morsel of your body, your wisdom, your kindness, your art, is another bid for perfection, a chance to get it right this time, or next time, or the time after that.

There is no death.

The beaching explains the variety of people coming at Jay from all directions, sudsing the surf. Some wear orange Gore-Tex, latex gloves, and goggles. Some wear the short-sleeved blue shirts and caps of the Dirty CGs. Some have insignias, NOAA, NMFS, local police. Others are in civilian wear, the onlookers who always show up to whale beachings, maybe even the boaters who heard the whale's vocal-fold shriek and alerted the beach crew that something was wrong.

The shedding of a robe: the whale's heart slips from Jay's naked feet.

He's floating on his back, carried along the water surface by a team of six. The ocean is purple with blood and yellow with whale fat. Jay gazes down at his body. He looks like a plastic doll chucked into a blender with bones and neoprene.

Jay thinks of Dad's scars: kid stuff.

And imagines the future tattoos that will tie his own scars together.

The *thwak* of lobtailing continues, dimmed beneath the splashes of boots through the rolling tide. No more heiliger Schauer. A diver's peace at last. Jay stares straight up. A scientist stares down through her goggles.

"What's your name, kid?"

He licks bloody lips. Uncertain if he's the same species.

"Come on. What's your name?"

Does he speak? Does he click?

"Do me a giant favor and tell me your name?"

Some holy books end on questions. But Jay's never been religious.

"Jay."

The woman smiles. She has a cherub's face.

"Hi, Jay. I'm Joy."

Yes, you are, Jay thinks.

"You're going to be fine, Jay."

Yes, I am, Jay thinks.

Fact: sperm whales sleep less than any mammal on Earth.

Jay, son of Mitt, son of whale, will follow suit.

His broken body joggles as one of the people carrying him makes the first hard step onto the beach. Solid ground. Cloudscape left behind. No abyss. Only mountains. Ocean eaten by beach, eaten by woods, eaten by road, eaten by forest, drunk down by the sky: a path of digestion, of appreciation. Each step existing by the grace of what has fallen and rotted before it.

Jay didn't find his dad's remains.

He *is* his dad's remains.

He breathes sleepy at last.

The whole of the bay lifts and shushes, the prehistoric rock and desperate kelp and larking sea life exhaling as one, a refrain, the first words Jay ever remembers hearing transformed from a frustrated father's complaint to a dad's inspiration, gauntlets Jay will need to face right here on the naked beach, and tomorrow plugged into hospital tubes, and the day after, and the day after that, and every day that life washes another whale into his path. The refrain is but two words: and the world is the comma between them.

3000 PSI

Sleeper, arise!

ACKNOWLEDGMENTS

Richard Abate, Tara Altebrando, Venus Azar, Spencer Beard, Bryan Bliss, Steve Brezenoff, Hannah Carande, Dan Chaon, Phil Clapham, Chuck Coursey, Brian Duffield, Adrian Durand, Joshua Ferris, Mike Ford, Connor Gallagher, Rebecca Giggs, Steven Haddock, Daniel Handler, Corey Ann Haydu, Elizabeth Hitti, Karlyn Hixson, Lara Horstmann, Gabino Iglesias, Melanie Iglesias, Zakiya Jamal, Stephen Graham Jones, P. Andrew Karam, Jennifer Kearney, Virginia Kemp, Owen King, Falon Kirby, Gretchen Koss, Amanda Kraus, Julia Leudtke, Judy Melinek, Carrie Mesrobian, Tom Mustill, Alissa Nutting, Craig Ouellette, Javier Ramirez, Joy Reidenberg, Mary Roach, Grant Rosenberg, Will Rowbotham, Phil Sammet, Julia Smith, Martha Stevens, Michael Taeckens, Christian Trimmer, Katharine Ulrich, Meg Walker, Brett Wean, Pat Webster, Michael Werle, Hal Whitehead, and Sara Zarr.

On the night of November 9, 2020, I was hanging out, socially distanced and cold, with my friends Mike Ford and Craig Ouellette. Because we stood on Chicago's Jarvis Beach—what is left of it after erosion—our conversation turned to a viral video of two kayakers, Julie McSorley and Liz Cottriel, nearly ending up in the mouth of a breaching humpback whale in San Luis Obispo Bay, California.

I watched it the next morning. The video pointed me toward other legends, none plausible, of people being swallowed alive by whales. Such tales crop up periodically, most recently with briefly famous lobster diver Michael Packard, who was carried in the mouth of a humpback whale for thirty seconds on June 11, 2021. Any headlines that claim Packard, or anyone else, has been "swallowed" are misleading. These unlucky people are only—"only"—mouthed before being spat back into the sea.

Within an hour of seeing the kayaker video, I emailed nonfiction writer Mary Roach to ask if any of her offbeat interviews had broached the possibility of someone literally being swallowed by a whale. Indeed, she'd touched on the subject in her book *Gulp*, and directed me to her source, Phil Clapham, senior scientist at Seastar Scientific, and former director of the Cetacean Assessment and Ecology Program at Seattle's National Marine Mammal Laboratory.

Phil told me that, while most whale throats are far too narrow to fit a human, a sperm whale's throat made it theoretically possible.

He promptly connected me with Lara Horstmann, associate professor of marine biology at the College of Fisheries and Ocean Sciences, and Joy Reidenberg, professor of anatomy at the Center for Anatomy and Functional Morphology, Icahn School of Medicine at Mount Sinai. Over countless emails, phone calls, and video calls, Phil, Lara, and Joy—my "whalies," I dubbed them—hurled their creative energies into my story. Their expertise forms the guts of this novel.

Along with specialists in diving, jellyfish, body decomposition, and much more, my whalies helped make this book as scientifically and biologically accurate as possible—though, as they often comforted me, sperm whales remain mysterious enough to lend me a degree of artistic license. Easily the most contentious part of this novel is the notion that an adult sperm whale larynx can be manipulated to emit a primal scream. This ability is theoretical and debated. Yet it was such a thematically appropriate notion that I couldn't help but include it.

Finally, I want to alert my science-minded readers that I purposefully avoided italicizing scientific names. Not only did the scientific italics wage war with my emphatic italics, but I came to regard scientific terminology as a special language and wished to bestow on it the elevated status of unitalicized esteem.

A few special thanks. Spencer Beard and Mike Ford took me scuba diving for the first time while Amanda Kraus took down observations. Connor Gallagher, professional diver and videographer, helped me choose Monastery Beach as the book's setting and videotaped himself, twice, making Jay Gardiner's dive to the precipice of Carmel Canyon, avoiding whale ingestion both times. Julia Leudtke gave me a basic understanding of the larynx (albeit human). P. Andrew Karam crunched through the arduous calculations required to realistically pull off the book's explosion. Will Staehle created the striking cover art. Christian Trimmer edited this book, as he has so many of my previous, with heart, sensitivity, and insight. There is no one better.

The eight books never more than two feet away from me were *Atlas of the Anatomy of Dolphins and Whales* by Stefan Huggenberger, Helmut Oelschläger, and Bruno Cozzi; *The Book of Jonah: A Social Justice Commentary* by Shmuly Yanklowitz; *Cannery Row* by John Steinbeck; *The Certified Diver's Handbook* by Clay Coleman; *Fathoms: The World in the Whale* by Rebecca Giggs; *The Great Sperm Whale* by Richard Ellis; *Sperm Whales: Social Evolution in the Ocean* by Hal Whitehead; and *Whales, Dolphins & Porpoises: A Natural History and Species Guide* by Annalisa Berta.

Despite this surfeit of scientific assistance, I am not a scientist. This cannot be stressed enough. All technical mistakes in this book must be considered my own.

RESOURCES

If you have lost a loved one to suicide, or know someone who has, you can find information about the American Foundation for Suicide Prevention's Healing Conversations program, International Survivors of Suicide Loss Day, and a listing of suicide loss support groups at afsp.org/get-help.

If you are in distress or want guidance on how to help someone who is, and live in the United States, you can find a complete list of crisis services, including specialized support for LGBTQ+ and underrepresented communities, at afsp.org/get-help. These resources include:

988 Suicide & Crisis Lifeline: Call 988, or visit 988lifeline.org.

Crisis Text Line: Text HOME to 741741 or visit crisistextline.org.

Seize the Awkward: This site empowers teens and young adults to reach out to and support their friends. Visit seizetheawkward.org.

Veterans Crisis Line: Reach caring, qualified responders with the Department of Veterans Affairs. Call 800-273-8255 and press 1, or visit veteranscrisisline.net.

You are also encouraged to connect with one of the American Foundation for Suicide Prevention's local chapters to find out about resources and events in your area, and to connect with others who understand at afsp.org/find-a-local-chapter/.

If you or someone you know is struggling with mental health, please visit mentalhealthishealth.us for resources and support.